Whether Or Not She Was Ready To Admit It, She'd Been As Turned On By That Hot, Sweet-Salty Kiss As He Was.

It occurred to him that he might have set his mission back a few days.

Or maybe not. Maybe now that he'd defused this crazy physical attraction, he could concentrate on doing what he'd come down here to do.

So there was some electricity sizzling between them. Roughly enough to light up Shea Stadium. It might help if he could take her to bed and make love until he was cross-eyed, but that wasn't going to happen.

It might also help if he could find whatever he was looking for and get the hell out—put a few hundred miles between them. But somewhere along the line, that idea had lost its appeal.

Dear Reader,

Thanks for choosing Silhouette Desire, where we bring you the ultimate in powerful, passionate and provocative love stories. Our immensely popular series DYNASTIES: THE BARONES comes to a rollicking conclusion this month with Metsy Hingle's *Passionately Ever After.* But don't worry, another wonderful family saga is on the horizon. Come back next month when Barbara McCauley launches DYNASTIES: THE DANFORTHS. Full of Southern charm—and sultry scandals—this is a series not to be missed!

The wonderful Dixie Browning is back with an immersing tale in *Social Graces.* And Brenda Jackson treats readers to another unforgettable—and unbelievably hot!—hero in *Thorn's Challenge.* Kathie DeNosky continues her trilogy about hard-to-tame men with the fabulous *Lonetree Ranchers: Colt.*

Also this month is another exciting installment in the TEXAS CATTLEMAN'S CLUB: THE STOLEN BABY series. Laura Wright pens a powerful story with *Locked Up With a Lawman*—I think the title says it all. And welcome back author Susan Crosby who kicks off her brand-new series, BEHIND CLOSED DOORS, with the compelling *Christmas Bonus, Strings Attached.*

With wishes for a happy, healthy holiday season,

Melissa Jeglinski

Melissa Jeglinski
Senior Editor, Silhouette Desire

Please address questions and book requests to:
Silhouette Reader Service
U.S.: 3010 Walden Ave., P.O. Box 1325, Buffalo, NY 14269
Canadian: P.O. Box 609, Fort Erie, Ont. L2A 5X3

DIXIE
BROWNING
Social Graces

Published by Silhouette Books
America's Publisher of Contemporary Romance

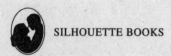

SILHOUETTE BOOKS

ISBN 0-373-76550-9

SOCIAL GRACES

Copyright © 2003 by Dixie Browning

This edition published by arrangement with Harlequin Books S.A.

® and TM are trademarks of Harlequin Books S.A., used under license.
Trademarks indicated with ® are registered in the United States Patent
and Trademark Office, the Canadian Trade Marks Office and in other
countries.

Visit Silhouette at www.eHarlequin.com

Printed in U.S.A.

DIXIE BROWNING

is an award-winning painter and writer, mother and grandmother who has written nearly eighty contemporary romances. Dixie and her sister, Mary Williams, also write historical romances as Bronwyn Williams. Contact Dixie at www.dixiebrowning.com, or at P.O. Box 1389, Buxton, NC 27920.

One

Standing in the middle of the bedroom, dangling a pair of Chanel slingbacks by the stiletto heels, with a sleeveless black Donna Karan slung over her shoulder, Val Bonnard stared at the partially open closet and listened for the scratching noise to come again. Shivering in the chill air, she glanced quickly at the window. With the wind howling a gale, it might be only a branch scraping the eaves. What else could it be? She was alone in the house, wasn't she?

She was alone, period.

Swallowing the lump that threatened to lodge permanently in her throat, she glared at the closet door. It was ajar because there wasn't a level surface in the entire house. All the doors swung open, and all the windows leaked cold air. The temperature outside hovered in the low forties, which wasn't particularly cold for Carolina in the middle of January, but it felt colder because of the wind. And the dampness.

And the aloneness.

She was still glaring when the mouse emerged, tipped her a glance, twitched its ears, then calmly proceeded to follow the baseboard to a postage-stamp-sized hole near the corner of the room.

It was the last straw in a haystack of last straws. Grief, anger and helplessness clotted around her and she dropped onto the edge of the sagging iron-framed bed and let the tears come.

A few minutes later she sniffed and felt in the pocket of her leather jeans for a tissue. As if pockets designed to display starbursts of rhinestones could possibly harbor anything so practical.

Sniffing again, she thought, it's not going to work. What on earth had she expected? That by driving for two days to reach a quaint, half remembered house on a half remembered barrier island she would not only escape from crank calls, but magically exchange grief for perspective? That a lightbulb would suddenly appear above her head and she would instantly know who was responsible for Bonnard Financial Consultants' downfall, her father's disgrace, his arrest and his untimely death?

Time and distance lent perspective. She'd read that somewhere, probably on a greeting card. She'd had more than two and a half months. Time hadn't helped.

As for distance, she had run as far away as she

could run, to the only place she had left. Now she was here with as many of her possessions as she could cram into her new, cheap, gas-guzzling secondhand car, in a village so small it lacked so much as a single stoplight. She had even escaped from those irritating calls, as there wasn't a working phone in the house. Her cell phone with its caller ID didn't seem to work here.

There wasn't a dry cleaner on the island either, and half her wardrobe required dry-cleaning, most of it special handling. "Why not whine about it, wimp?" she muttered.

At least focusing on trivia helped stave off other thoughts—thoughts that swept her too close to the edge.

It had taken all her energy since her father had died to settle his affairs and dispose of the contents of the gabled, slate-roofed Tudor house that had been home for most of her life. Although stunned to learn that it was so heavily mortgaged, she'd actually been relieved when the bank had taken over the sale.

The rest had gone quickly—the disposal of the contents. Belinda and Charlie had helped enormously before they'd moved to take on new positions. She and Belinda had shared more than a few tears, and even stoic old Charlie had been red-eyed a few times.

In the end, all she'd brought south with her was her hand luggage, three garment bags and three banana boxes, one filled with personal mementos, one with linens, and another with the files she'd retrieved from her father's study.

In retrospect, everything about the past eleven weeks had been unreal in the truest sense of the word. There'd been a bottle of special vintage Moët Chandon in the industrial-sized, stainless-steel refrigerator, waiting for her birthday celebration. Her father had bought it the day before he'd been arrested. "Belinda has orders to prepare all your favorite dishes," he'd told her the night before, looking almost cheerful for a change. The old lines and shadows had been there, but at least there'd been some color in his face.

She'd asked several times before if anything was worrying him. Each time he'd brushed off her question. "Stock market's down," he'd said the last time, then he'd brightened. "Cholesterol's down, too, though. Can't have everything, can we?"

She'd chided him for spending too much time downtown and been relieved when he'd promised to take her advice and start spending more time at home, even though she knew very well he would spend most of it closed up in his study with *Forbes* and the *Wall Street Journal.*

For her birthday she had deliberately arranged to have dinner at home with only her dad instead of the usual bash at the club. She had planned to mellow him with the champagne and find out exactly what had been eating at him. But early on the morning of her thirtieth birthday a pair of strangers who turned out to be police officers had shown up at the door and invited her father to accompany them downtown. She'd seen the whole thing from the top of the stairs. Barefoot and wearing only a robe and night-gown, she had hurried downstairs, demanding to know what was happening.

The spokesman for the pair had been stiffly polite. "Just a few questions, miss, that's all." But obviously that hadn't been all. Her father had been ashen. Alarmed, she'd called first his physician, then his lawyer.

The next few hours had swept past like a kaleidoscope. She didn't recall having gotten dressed—she certainly hadn't taken time to shower, much less to arrange her hair before racing outside. Belinda had called after her and told her to take her father's medicine to the police station, so she'd dashed back and snatched the pill bottle from the housekeeper's hand.

They'd had only brief minutes to speak privately when the officer in the room with him had gone to get him a cup of water. Speaking quietly, as if he were afraid of being overheard, Frank Bonnard had instructed her to remove all unlabeled paper files from the file cabinet in his study and store them in her bedroom.

Confused and frightened, she had wanted to ask more, but just then the officer had returned. Her father had nodded, swallowed his pills and said, "Go home. I'll be there as soon as I get through here."

That was the last time she'd seen him alive. Before he could even be bonded out, he'd suffered a fatal coronary.

Now, peeling a paper towel from the roll on the old oak dresser, Val blew her nose, mopped her eyes and sighed. She'd been doing entirely too much of that lately. Great, gasping sighs, as if she were starved for oxygen.

What she was starved for were answers. Now that it was too late, she wondered if it had been a mistake to leave Greenwich. She could have rented a room, possibly even an apartment. If there were any answers to be found, they would hardly be found halfway down the East Coast in a tiny village her father had visited only once in his entire life.

On the other hand, the auditors, the men from the Financial Crimes Unit, plus those from all the various government agencies involved, were convinced they already had their man—their scapegoat—even though they'd made another token arrest. And even if she were to unravel the mess and prove beyond a shadow of a doubt that her father was innocent, it was too late to bring him back. The best she could hope to do was to restore his reputation.

Light from the setting sun, filtered by ancient, moss-draped live oaks, turned the dusty windows opaque. So many things on the island had changed since she'd last seen this old house, she would never have found it without the real estate agent's explicit instruction.

Just over a week ago she had called the agency that managed the property she'd inherited from her great-grandmother, Achsah Dozier. A few hours ago, following the agent's instructions, she had located Seaview Realty. While the office was scarcely larger than a walk-in closet, the woman seated behind a desk cluttered with brochures, boxes of Girl Scout cookies and what appeared to be tax forms, seemed friendly, if somewhat harried.

"Marian Kuvarky." The woman nodded toward the nameplate on her desk. "Glad you made it before I had to close up," she said, handing over a set of keys. "I'd better warn you, though—I still haven't found anyone to give the place a good going-over since the people who were renting it moved out. You might want to check into a motel for a few days."

Val had come too far to be put off another moment. Besides, she couldn't afford a motel. Even in the dead of winter, beach prices would seriously erode her dwindling funds. "I can take care of a little dirt, just tell me how to find my house." She was hardly helpless. She had looked after a three-room apartment with only a weekly maid before she'd moved back home to Connecticut.

Ms. Kuvarky, a youngish blonde with tired eyes and an engaging smile said, "Okay, but don't say I didn't warn you. Take a left once you leave here and turn off onto the Back Road."

"What's the name of it?"

"Of what?"

"The road."

"Back Road. It's named that. I had the power turned on after you called. I forgot if I told you or not, but the last renters left owing for two months. I would have had it ready to rent out again once I found somebody to do a few minor repairs, but like I said over the phone, my cleaner's out on maternity leave. She says she'll be back, but you know how that goes. I'm sort of coasting for now, trying to get through the slack season. I cleaned two places myself last weekend.''

Val had been too tired to involve herself in the agent's problems. Her stomach hadn't stood the trip well, as she'd nibbled constantly on junk food, more from nerves than from hunger. ''I brought linens. You said the house was furnished,'' she reminded Ms. Kuvarky.

The agent had nodded. ''Pretty much all you'll need, I guess, but it's sort of a mishmash. I wrote to your father about the repairs—those are extra—but I never heard back. Anyway, there's so much construction going on these days, even between seasons, it's hard to find dependable help.''

Ms. Kuvarky had promised to call around. Val remembered thinking that if the place had a roof and a bed, everything else could wait.

Now she wasn't quite so sure.

The last thing the rental agent had said as Val had stood in the doorway, trying to get her bearings in a village that had nothing even faintly resembling city blocks or even village squares, was ''By the way, if you happen to be looking for work and know one end of a broom from the other, you're hired.''

She'd been joking, of course. It might even come to that, Val told herself now, but at the moment she had other priorities. Starting with getting rid of her resident mouse.

* * *

The power was on, that was the good part. The bad part was that there was no phone. Or maybe that was the good part, too. A few crank calls had even managed to get through call-blocking before she'd left Greenwich, but they could hardly follow her to a place where she didn't have a working phone.

There was no central heat, only an oil heater in the living room and an assortment of small space heaters scattered in the other rooms. She'd managed to turn the oil heater on. The thing hadn't exploded, so she assumed she'd pushed the right button.

The water heater was another matter. She let the hot water faucet run for five minutes, but luke was as warm as it got. That's when she'd discovered that her cell phone didn't work. She'd tried to call Ms. Kuvarky, and the darned thing blanked out on her. No signal.

All right, so she would think of herself as a pioneer woman. At least she had a bed to sleep in instead of a covered wagon somewhere in the middle of the wilderness. She was thirty years old, with a degree from an excellent college—and although she was somewhat out of her element at the moment, she'd never been accused of being a slow learner. However, repairing major household appliances just might stretch her capability close to the breaking point. Sooner or later—probably sooner—she would have to look for a paying job in order to hire someone to do the things she couldn't figure out how to do herself.

One thing she definitely could do was clean her

house. That accomplished, she could start going through her father's files, looking for whatever he'd wanted her to find that would enable his lawyer to reopen his case posthumously and clear his name.

There *had* to be something there. Otherwise, why had he made that strange, hurried request? He could've had no way of knowing that he'd be dead within hours of being arrested.

Bitter? Yes, she was bitter. But grief and bitterness weren't going to solve any problems, either those facing her here or those she'd left behind.

She stood, crossed the small room and kicked at the baseboard. "All right, Mickey, your time is up. Sorry, but I'm not in a sharing mood, so pack up your acorns or whatever and move out."

By no standards was the house she'd inherited from Achsah Dozier comparable to the one she'd left behind. The original structure might have been modernized at some point since she'd last seen it, but the white paint was peeling rather badly and a few of the faded green shutters dangled from single hinges.

At least the gingerbread trim on the front eaves was intact. She remembered thinking in terms of a fairy tale when she'd been told as a child that the fancy trim was called gingerbread. The fact that her great-grandmother had actually baked gingerbread that day, the spicy scent greeting them at the front door, had only enhanced the illusion.

Marian Kuvarky had mentioned that a few years before she'd died, Achsah Dozier had had part of the old back porch turned into another bedroom and bare-bones bath with its own separate entrance, in case she needed live-in help. Since her death, it had occasionally been rented separately. Val briefly considered the possibility and decided that she wasn't cut out to play landlady.

On the other hand, unearned income was not to be sneezed at.

Dropping the shoes and dress she'd been clutching, she headed downstairs in search of cleaning materials. Before she could even consider sleeping in the room, she had to do something about the mice-and-mildew smell, either air it out or scrub it out. It was too cold to air it out.

It occurred to her that if Ms. Kuvarky had any idea of just how little she knew about the domestic arts, she would never have offered her a job cleaning houses, even as a joke.

Later that evening Val stepped out of the rust-stained, claw-footed upstairs bathtub onto a monogrammed hand towel. She hadn't bothered to pack such things as tablecloths, dresser scarves or bath mats, knowing that short of renting a trailer, she had to draw the line somewhere.

She had augmented the lukewarm water with a kettle of boiling water brought up from the kitchen. One kettle wasn't enough, but by the time she'd heated another one, the first would be cold, so she'd settled for lukewarm and quick.

Now, covered in goose bumps, she swaddled her damp body in a huge bath towel. Aside from being grimy and smelly, the house was also drafty. There was a space heater between the tub and the lavatory that helped as long as she didn't move more than a foot away from the glowing element. At least with all the drafts, carbon monoxide wouldn't be a problem. As for the danger of an electrical fire, that was another matter.

Note: have the water heater repaired.
Note: have the wiring checked.

Which reminded her—what about insurance?

"Welcome to the real world, Ms. Bonnard," she whispered a few minutes later, flipping an 800-count Egyptian-cotton king-sized bottom sheet over the sagging double-bed mattress.

She'd pulled on a pair of navy satin pajamas, a Peruvian hand-knit sweater jacket and a pair of slipper socks. January or not, wasn't this supposed to be the sunny south?

Fortunately, she'd crammed two down-filled duvets in around her suitcases, one of which she'd immediately tossed over the ugly brown plaid sofa downstairs. The other one was miles too large for the double bed, but its familiar paisley cover was comforting. That done, she collected a pen and notepad and settled down for some serious list making, ignoring the reminder from her stomach that except for pretzels, popcorn and two candy bars, she hadn't eaten since breakfast. Starting early tomorrow she had a million things to do to make this place even marginally livable before she could concentrate on searching her father's files for evidence of his innocence.

Nibbling the white-tipped cap of her Mont Blanc, she reread the shopping list. Table cloth—one had standards, after all. Mattress cover—she definitely didn't like the looks of that mattress, even after she'd flipped it. Oh, and a bath mat. She'd have to ask where to buy linens here on the island.

On to the next list. Tea, bagels, other foods, preferably already prepared. Wrinkling her nose, she added mousetraps to the list. And cleaning supplies.

A clean house was something she'd always taken for granted. After graduating from college she'd lived in small apartments, first in Chicago, then in Manhattan—always in upscale neighborhoods. She had moved back to her father's house after he'd suffered his first small stroke, and soon after that she'd gotten involved with a few of the local charities. It was what she did best, after all—manage fund-raisers for worthy causes. She had frequently acted as her father's hostess, although most of his business entertaining had been done at the club.

Looking back, it had been a comfortable way to coast through life. Not particularly exciting—no major achievements—but certainly comfortable.

"Definitely room for improvement," she murmured, her voice echoing hollowly in the old house.

Tired, hungry, but oddly energized, she surveyed her surroundings. Gone were the familiar French wallpaper in her old bedroom, the mismatched but well-cared-for semi-antique furniture, the faded oriental rug and her eclectic art collection. Here she was confronted by gritty bare floors, dark with layers of varnish—naked, white-painted walls, dusty windows, and the lingering aroma of mouse spoor.

Okay. She could handle that. The sand, she'd quickly discovered, hid in the cracks between the floorboards so that each time she went over it with a broom, more appeared. She could live with a little sand. This was the beach, after all. Even if she couldn't see the ocean from here, she could hear it.

She added window spray and bathroom cleaner to the list, hoping there would be directions on the bottles in case she got into trouble. More paper towels. Sponges. Rubber gloves, although she probably wouldn't be able to wear them without her hands breaking out. Her skin was inclined to be sensitive.

Note: take down the for rent sign on the front lawn.

The lawn itself was a mess, but once she was through scrubbing the entire house, maybe she could paint the front door a bright color to deflect attention from that and the rest of the peeling paint until she could afford to landscape and repaint the entire house. There was nothing wrong with old, but she preferred old and charming to old and neglected.

One more note: find position that pays in advance.

Leaning back on the two down-filled pillows, she closed her eyes. "Dad, what am I going to do?" she whispered. "Charlie, Belinda—Miss Mitty, where are you when I need you?"

The only sound was the plaintive honking of a flock of wild geese flying overhead. It was barely nine o'clock. She *never* went to bed before eleven, often not until the small hours of the morning.

Her last memory before sleep claimed her was of her father being led outside to an unmarked car while she stood in the doorway, too stunned even to protest. One of the officers pressed her father's head down and urged him into the back seat.

It had been Sunday, the morning of her birthday. Belinda had made blueberry pancakes for breakfast. Frank Bonnard, an early riser, had evidently been in his study. He'd been dressed in flannels, an open-necked white shirt and a navy Shetland sweater when Charlie had answered the door. Val remembered thinking much later that if the ghouls could have stuffed him into a pair of orange coveralls before marching him out in front of the single reporter who had probably tuned in on the police radio and followed them to the Belle Haven address, they'd have done it.

That had been only the beginning. Within hours, the press had swarmed like locusts. Shortly after that the phone calls had started. Despite all the blocking devices, a few people managed to get through with variations ranging from "Where's my money?" to "Frank Bonnard owes me my pension, dammit. Where is it? What am I supposed to do now?"

The calls had ended when the police had put taps

on all three phone lines. Not until recently had she wondered why they'd ceased. How could the callers have known their calls could be traced?

The calls had stopped, but not the nightmares. Both asleep and awake, she had replayed the scene that morning back in late September a thousand times. A pale, stiff-faced Charlie stepping back from the wide front door to allow the two men inside. Her father emerging from his study and carefully closing the door behind him. Belinda, one plump hand covering her mouth as she stood in the dining-room doorway.

In less than twelve hours her father had been dead. Pestered by reporters, auditors and men in bad suits who seemed to think they had every right to invade her home, Val had tried desperately to cram her emotions deep inside her and lock the door. When confronted, she'd quickly learned to answer with one of several replies that included, "I don't know," "No comment," and "My father is innocent."

A part of her was still in hiding, but she had to know the truth, even in the unlikely event that the truth turned out to be not what she wanted to hear. Back in Greenwich she'd been too close for any real objectivity. Here, once she settled down to it, she would be able to think clearly. Then at least the callers who wanted to know where their money was would have an answer, even if it was one that wouldn't do them any good.

Valerie Bonnard slept heavily that night. Sometime before daybreak she awoke, thinking about the mouse she'd seen and all the others she'd heard and smelled. Were mice carnivorous? They were grain-eaters, weren't they?

Oh, God…now she'd never get back to sleep.

Eyes scrunched tightly shut, she rolled over onto her stomach. On her own firm, pillow-top mattress, prone had been her favorite sleeping position, never mind that her face would be a mass of wrinkles by the time she reached forty. On a mattress that sagged like a hammock, it was a toss-up as to which she'd succumb to first—strangulation or a broken back.

Grax, if this was your bed, no wonder your back was rounded, she thought guiltily. Her great-grandmother's given name had been Achsah, pronounced *Axa.* As a child, Val had shortened it to Grax. From her one brief visit, she remembered the old woman with the laughing blue eyes and short white hair. Wearing a duckbill cap, a cotton print dress and tennis shoes, she'd been working in the yard when they'd driven up. On their way to Hilton Head, her parents had taken a detour along the Outer Banks so that Lola, Val's mother, could introduce them to her grandmother.

To a child of seven, the trip had seemed endless. Her parents had bickered constantly in the front seat. Odd that she should remember that now. Looking back, it seemed as if it had been her mother who was reluctant to take the time, not her father.

They'd spent the night at a motel, but they'd eaten dinner in the small white house in the woods. She remembered thinking even before she'd smelled the gingerbread that it looked like Aunty Em's house in the Wizard of Oz.

Grax had served boiled fish—she'd called it drum—mixed with mashed potatoes, raw onions and bits of crisp fried salt pork. As strange as it sounded, it had turned out to be an interesting mixture of flavors and textures.

Her mother hadn't touched it. Her father had sampled a few forkfuls. Val, for reasons she could no longer recall, had cleaned off her plate and bragged excessively. She'd eaten two squares of the gingerbread with lemon sauce that had followed.

That had been both the first and the last time she'd seen her great-grandmother. Two years later her parents had separated. Her father had been given custody—had her mother even asked? At any rate, Lola Bonnard had chosen to live abroad for the next few years, so visitation had been out of the question. Val had gone through the usual stages of wondering if the split had been her fault and scheming to bring her parents together again.

She would like to think her mother had attended Grax's funeral but she really didn't know that, either. Her relationship with Lola Bonnard had never been close, even before the divorce. Since then it had dwindled to an exchange of Christmas cards and the occasional birthday card. It had been her father's lawyer who'd handled Grax's bequest, arranging for someone to manage the house as a rental. At the time, Val had been living in Chicago working for a private foundation that funded shelters and basic health services for runaway girls.

"I'm sorry, Grax," she whispered now, burdened with a belated sense of guilt. "I'm embarrassed and sorry and I hope you had lots and lots of friends so that you didn't really miss us."

No wonder the house felt so cold and empty. How many strangers had lived here since Grax had died? There was nothing of Achsah Dozier left, no echoes of the old woman's island brogue that had fascinated Val at the time. No hint of the flowers she'd brought inside from the Cape jasmine bushes that had once bloomed in her yard. Lola had complained about the cloying scent and without a word, Grax had got up and set the vase on the back porch.

Val made a silent promise that as soon as she got the house cleaned and repaired, she would see what could be done with the yard.

But first she had to go through those files, discover what it was her father had wanted her to find there, and clear his name. Frank Bonnard had been a good man, an honest man, if something of an impractical dreamer. He didn't deserve what had happened to him.

Two

John Leo MacBride studied the encrusted mass of plates and cutlery that had been brought up from one of the Nazi submarines sunk during the Second World War off the New England coast. He considered leaving a few as he'd found them instead of soaking them all in an acid solution, prying them apart and cleaning them up. The before-and-after contrast would make a far more interesting display at the small museum that had commissioned the dives.

He glanced at the clock on the wall of his stepbrother's garage where he'd set up a temporary workspace a couple of months ago when Will had called, asking for help. So far, about all he'd been able to do was to keep Macy, Will's wife, from making matters worse. That and stay on the heels of his lawyer, who might as well be back chasing ambulances for all the good he'd done his client.

Mac had been standing by chiefly to offer moral support, which was more than Macy was doing. Instead, she seemed almost to be enjoying her role as the wife of a man who was currently awaiting trial for embezzlement. She'd had her hair highlighted two days after Will had made bail, and since then had managed to get a fair amount of facetime with the media.

Bonnard's daughter, by contrast, had avoided the worst of the feeding frenzy. He could think of a couple of reasons why she might have managed to avoid the spotlight, but social clout didn't mean her old man wasn't guilty as sin.

Will's only crime, Mac was convinced of it, was being too trusting. Less than a year after being given a partnership, Will had gone down in the corporate shipwreck along with Frank Bonnard, founder and CEO of the privately held financial consulting firm. Bonnard had paid for his sins by dying of a massive heart attack almost before the investigation got underway.

Will had hired an inept lawyer—an old law-school classmate. A lawyer himself, as well as a CPA, he'd been planning to present his own defense when Mac had talked him out of it. He was sorry now that he had.

But the money was still missing, and after nearly three months, the trail was murkier than ever. Current thinking was that funds had been bled off gradually over a period of years rather than months, probably funneled from one offshore account to another until it was impossible to trace either the source or the destination.

No one was talking. Bonnard because he was dead, Will because he was clueless, his lawyer because if the jerk had ever passed a bar, it wasn't a bar that served drinks. The guy was a lush.

Mac had tried his own brand of logic on the case, running down the short list of suspects. The Chief Financial Officer, Sam Hutchinson, had apparently been cleared. Currently on an extended leave of absence to be with his terminally ill wife, he'd been the logical suspect. His computers, his files—everything that bore his fingerprints, had been impounded. He'd come through it all clean. Will liked the guy. Only hours before he'd died, Bonnard himself had vouched for him.

As for Bonnard, late founder and CEO of Bonnard Financial Consultants, not even death had offered protection. Once the flock of outside auditors dug in, both he and Will had been swept up in the dragnet.

It was shortly after that that Mac had moved his base of operations from an apartment in Mystic, near the aquarium, to Will's Greenwich home. He was currently living in the small apartment over the garage, finishing up a few tasks from his last commissioned dive.

BFC was a small regional firm, nothing like some of the big outfits that had hit the reef over the past few years. Not that the impact on the victims was any less devastating, as BFC had specialized in handling retirement funds for a number of small area businesses.

To give him credit, back when the economy had taken a dive a few years ago, Bonnard had borrowed heavily against his fancy house and pumped the funds back into the company, a fact that had quickly come to light. It didn't exactly fit the profile of a high-level embezzler to Mac's way of thinking, unless at the same time he'd been shoring up the business with one hand to allay suspicions, he'd been bleeding off profits with the other. Slick trick, if you could pull it off.

Bonnard's only heir was a daughter. The feds had run her through the washer just as a precaution, but so far as anyone knew she had never been involved in any way with her father's business. Will was convinced she wasn't a player.

Will's wife, Macy, wasn't so generous, but then, Macy was inclined to be jealous of any attractive woman, especially one who'd been born with the proverbial silver spoon. Even Mac had to wonder if the investigators had gone easy on the daughter because of her looks and her social position. He wasn't sure how big a part sympathy played in such a case, but the fact that her father had died on his daughter's thirtieth birthday might have had an effect. The press had made it a big deal. He remembered seeing that same pale, stricken face—flawless cheekbones, haunted gray eyes—replayed over and over on every recount during the week immediately after Bonnard's arrest—an arrest that had been followed almost immediately by his death.

Ironic to think that Bonnard might have got clean away if it hadn't been for a junior accountant who had mistakenly mailed out 1099s for a tax-free municipal fund to a number of clients and been forced to do amended forms. Evidently the matter had landed on the desk of a snarky IRS agent. One question had led to another; an outside auditor had been called in, and the whole house of cards had come crashing down. Bonnard had gone to his dubious reward, leaving his junior partner to take the fall.

That's when the scavenger hunt had shifted into high gear, drawing in the FBI, the Financial Crimes Unit, the state auditor's department and the IRS, not to mention a bunch of media types with Woodward and Bernstein complexes. But with all that manpower, they were no closer after nearly three months to locating the missing money, much less tracing it back to its source.

Which damn well wasn't Will Jordan.

Mac's single bag was packed, the Land Cruiser's tank topped off. He was ready to head south the minute Shirley, his hacker friend, gave the word. Not that hacking was even needed in this case, as public records were open to everyone who knew, geographically speaking, where to look. But when he needed information in a hurry, it helped to know someone who could make a computer sit up and sing the "Star Spangled Banner."

Valerie Bonnard's only asset of record at this moment was a modest trust fund that wouldn't kick in for another five years, and a small property she'd inherited in a place called Buxton, on North Carolina's Outer Banks. Mac was generally familiar with the area—what marine archeologist wasn't familiar with the notorious Graveyard of the Atlantic? There was even a new museum by that name on the island. From what he'd been able to find on the Internet, most of the island that hadn't been taken over by Park Service or National Wildlife had been developed over the past few decades.

Ms. Bonnard, using a dummy corporation, could have been investing steadily in some high-dollar real estate down there. Shirley hadn't been able to tie her to anything specific, but it would have been a smart move on the part of La Bonnard, especially considering the erratic stock market. Whether or not she'd socked away the missing funds in investment-grade real estate, it was as good a place to start as any.

One of the perks of being a freelance marine archeologist was large chunks of unregulated time. Unlike Will's, Mac's lifestyle was both portable and low maintenance, although Will's was probably about to change even more drastically in the near future. Mac had a feeling that once this nightmare was over, his stepbrother might have lost more than a junior partnership, an upscale house and a few club memberships. Macy was looking restless now that the publicity had died down. She just might walk, which would be no great loss in Mac's estimation.

* * *

The drive took two days, allowing for frequent breaks, in his fourteen-year-old, rebuilt Land Cruiser. Mac spent the first night in the Norfolk region. Late in the afternoon of the second day, having spent a few hours in one of the area's maritime museums, he pulled into a motel in Buxton and booked a room, intending to spend the first half hour flexing various muscles under a hot shower.

At age thirty-seven he was beginning to realize that stick shifts were hell on left knees. A friend had warned him, but he wasn't about to trade in his customized vehicle, with the locked compartments designed specifically to hold his diving gear and the ergonomic seats that helped minimize fatigue. It might take him a bit longer to bounce back after a long drive, but normally he looked on the bounce-back time as a chance to catch up on his reading. He'd even tossed in a few books at the last minute, in case he had any down time. Not that he planned to hang around any longer than it took to uncover a lead that would shift the focus off Will.

If Mac had a weakness—actually, he admitted to several—it was books. Aside from diving gear, books were his favorite indulgence. Mostly history. The stuff fascinated him, always had. But reading could wait until he'd pinned the Bonnard woman down and got the information he needed.

A fleeting image of him pinning La Bonnard down on a big, soft bed drifted across his field of vision. He blinked it away before it could take root.

The desk clerk was young and inclined to be chatty. It took Mac all of two minutes to get the location of the residence of the late Achsah Dozier, as this wasn't the kind of place where street addresses did much good.

"I didn't really know her, I've only been here a few years," the young woman said. She'd looked him over and touched her hair when he'd walked into the lobby, but evidently decided on closer examination that he wasn't that interesting.

Not altogether surprising. He still had all his hair and teeth, and he'd been asked more than once if he worked out at a gym. He didn't. The type of work he did tended to develop the legs and upper body while it pared down the waist and hips. On the other hand, his face had once been compared to a rockslide.

Besides, he had a couple of decades on the bubblegum-chewing kid, who was saying, "I think Miss Achsah used to live on the Back Road."

In certain pockets of population, he'd learned, *Miss* was an honorary title given to women over a certain age, regardless of marital status. When the first name was used, it generally indicated that there were a number of women with the same surname.

"You go out the door and turn left—" The young clerk continued to talk while Mac mentally recorded the data. "I heard her house was rented out after she died, but I don't think there's anybody living there now. Marian Kuvarky over at Seaview Realty could tell you."

Something—call it a hunter's instinct—told him that the Bonnard woman was holed up in her great-grandmother's house, probably keeping a low profile until things cooled down. If she had a brain under all that glossy black hair she had to know she was probably still considered "of interest" by certain authorities, even if they hadn't found anything to hold her on.

The smart thing would have been to go someplace where she had no ties and wait until the heat died down. After say, six months—a year would be even better—with what she had stashed away in an off-shore account, she could settle anywhere in the world.

With what she *allegedly* had stashed away, he corrected himself reluctantly. So far, he was the only one doing the alleging, but then, he had a personal stake. Will hadn't embezzled a damned thing. In the first place, his stepbrother couldn't lie worth crap, and in the second place, if he could've got his hands on that kind of money, his wife would've already spent it. Macy could easily qualify for the world shopping playoffs.

Mac was good at extrapolations. As a marine archeologist, it was what he did best. Study the evidence—the written records, plus any prevailing conditions, political or weatherwise, that might affect where a ship had reportedly gone down. Not until he had thoroughly examined all available data and given his instincts time to mull it over was he ready to home in on his target.

In this case the field had officially narrowed to two suspects: Bonnard and Will. Eliminate Will and that left only Bonnard—or in this case, Bonnard's heir. The auditors were still digging halfheartedly, but the case had been shoved to the back burner as new and bigger cases had intervened in the meantime. Which left poor Will dangling in the wind, his next hearing not even on the docket yet.

Mac made up his mind to wait until morning to scope out the house. He even might wait another day before making contact, but no longer than that. He needed answers. Will wasn't holding up well. He'd lost weight, he had circles under his eyes the size of hubcaps, and his marriage was falling apart.

Timing was crucial. He didn't want to spook her, but neither could he afford to wait too long. The feds hadn't been able to find anything to hold her on, not even as a witness, but to Mac, the logic was inescapable. That damned money hadn't just gone up in smoke. Someone close to Bonnard held the key. The man had been divorced more than twenty years; he'd never remarried. So far as anyone knew, he'd never even had a mistress. A few brief liaisons, but none that had lasted more than a few months. The press had gone after the ex-wife, now reportedly in the process of shedding husband number three. There was no love lost between her and Bonnard, so if she'd known anything it would probably have come out. Another dead end.

By process of elimination, it had to be the daughter. Millions of bucks didn't just slip through a crack in the floor like yellow dust in a gold-rush saloon. Someone was waiting for the heat to die down to claim it. And he knew who the most logical someone was.

Valerie Stevens Bonnard, Mac mused. He knew what she looked like, even knew what make car she drove. He'd seen her around town a couple of times when he'd been in the area visiting Will last spring. Cool, flawless—sexy in a touch-me-not way. Talk about your oxymorons.

He'd even spoken to her once. Will had gone to some BFC function at the country club while Mac was spending a few days in Greenwich on his way back from DC last summer. He'd forgotten his prescription sunglasses and called to asked Mac to drop them off.

Mac had been changing the fluid in his transmission when he'd answered the phone and hadn't bothered to change clothes, intending to leave the sunglasses with an attendant. Driving the same weathered Land Cruiser, he had just squeezed into a parking place between a Lexus and an Escalade when Ms. Bonnard drove up in Mercedes convertible. Evidently she'd mistaken him for one of the groundskeepers, because she'd informed him politely that service parking was in the rear. She'd even smiled, her big gray-green eyes about as warm as your average glacier.

So yeah, he knew what she looked like. There was no chance she would recognize him now though.

She'd summed him up and dismissed him in less than two seconds flat.

* * *

Val was good at any number of things, among them organizing intimate dinner parties for fifty people and overseeing thousand-dollar-a-plate fundraisers. She excelled at tennis, skiing and hanging art shows. She'd been drilled in what was expected of someone with her privileged background from the time she could walk.

Now, faced with an oven that was lined with three inches of burned-on gunk she burst into tears, only because cursing was not yet among her talents.

She wiped her eyes, smearing a streak of grime across her cheek and glared at the rattling kitchen window. There had to be a way to keep the wind from whipping in through the frames. How had the previous tenants managed to stay warm?

They hadn't, of course. Probably why they'd moved out, leaving the place in such a mess. Three of the rooms had air-conditioner units hanging out the windows. No one had bothered to remove or even to cover them, much less plug all the cracks around them. She had stuffed the cracks with the plastic bags from her first shopping foray, for all the good it did.

Neither the space heaters nor the ugly brown oil heater were a match for the damp chill that seemed to creep through the very walls. Hadn't anyone in the South ever heard of insulation?

She added a roll of clear plastic and a staple gun to the growing shopping list that included more of the sudsy cleanser, another six-pack of paper towels and a few more mousetraps. The plastic would have to serve until she could afford storm windows.

After hours spent scrubbing, most of the downstairs rooms plus her bedroom and the upstairs bath smelled of pine cleanser instead of mice and mildew. She'd ended up buying live traps instead of wire traps, even though they'd cost more, because while she refused to share her new home with rodents, she wasn't into killing. Spiders, roaches and mosquitoes, perhaps, but nothing larger.

Her new lifestyle, she was rapidly discovering, called for a drastically new mindset. Belinda and Charlie, her father's housekeeper and man-of-all-work, had spoiled her, she'd be the first to admit. Now, instead of taking her comfort for granted, she was forced to acquire a whole battery of new skills. In the process she was also acquiring an impressive array of bruises, splinters and broken fingernails, not to mention a rash on her left hand from the rubber gloves she'd tried to wear. French manicures and sleek hairstyles were definitely things of the past. After the second day, she hadn't bothered to apply makeup, only a quick splash of moisturizer and, when she remembered it, lip balm. Instead of her usual chignon, she wore her hair in a single braid that, by day's end, was usually frazzled and laced with cobwebs—or worse.

On the plus side, she was too busy to waste time crying. Hard work was turning out to be a fair remedy for grief. Somewhat surprisingly she was even

making a few friends. Marian Kuvarky at the real
estate office, the clerk at the hardware store who had
advised her on mousetraps, and the friendly woman
at the post office where she'd rented a mailbox.
She'd asked questions of all of them, everything
from where to find what on the island to what kind
of weather to expect.

"Expect the unexpected, I guess," the postal
worker had said, "This time of year we might get
seventy-five degrees one day and thirty-five the next.
Not much snow, but lawsy, the winds'll sandblast
your windshield before you know it. By the way, did
I tell you that you have to come here to collect your
mail? None of the villages on the island has home
delivery."

Which reminded her—she needed to get started
mailing change-of-address notices now that she had
an official address.

But first she had to finish scrubbing the tops of the
kitchen cabinets. She'd given up on the oven for
now—didn't know how to use the darned thing, anyway. But sooner or later she was going to defeat that
thick black crust if she had to resort to dynamite.

Once she finished the kitchen she would tackle the
back bedroom and bath in case she got desperate
enough to look for a tenant. Meanwhile she needed
to take down that half-hidden sign in the front yard.
Or maybe just cover it for the time being. While she
hated the idea of compromising her privacy, it might
be a way of bringing in an income until she could

look for work. Marian's offer of a job cleaning houses had been a joke...hadn't it?

Standing on the next-to-the-top step of the rickety stepladder she'd retrieved from a shed in the backyard, Val steadied herself by draping one arm over an open cabinet door while she wiped off the last section of cabinet top, wincing as her shoulder muscles protested. Hard to believe that only a few months ago she'd thought nothing of dancing all night, playing tennis all morning and spending the afternoon hanging a benefit art exhibit.

At least she no longer had trouble sleeping. A fast warm shower, a couple of acetominaphen caplets and she was out like a light. Over the past few months she'd lost count of all the nights she had lain awake, tunneling through endless caverns in search of answers that continued to elude her. Answers to questions such as, who could possibly have embezzled so much money without anyone's noticing in a small firm that was bristling with accountants? Oh, she'd heard all about the fancy shell games—most of them actually legal—that were played by some of the largest accounting firms. The fact remained, why hadn't anyone noticed until it was too late? What had happened to the money?

And why on earth hadn't she gone for an MBA instead of wasting her time on folk music, literature and art history?

Although, not even a Harvard MBA had kept her father from being taken in. But then, Frank Bonnard's strength had been pulling ideas out of the blue, working out an overall plan and counting on a select team to carry out the details. The team in this case had consisted of Sam Hutchinson, who'd been gone practically the whole year, and therefore couldn't have been involved, and the administrative assistant whom she'd never met before the woman had been asked to leave. Val had a feeling Miss Mitty might have engineered that, as evidently the newcomer had encroached on territory the older woman considered hers alone.

And of course, there was Will Jordan, the new junior partner who'd been indicted along with her father. He was probably guilty. The prosecutors must have thought so, as he was still out on bond.

To be fair she had to include Miss Mitty, longtime family friend and her father's efficient and insightful, if unofficial assistant. Not that she was in any way a suspect, but Mitty Stoddard had been there from the beginning. If she hadn't retired back in August she'd have known precisely where to start digging. While she might not have a college degree, much less a title, the woman was smarter than any of the younger members of the team gave her credit for being, Val was convinced of it.

Val made a mental note to try again to reach her. She'd dialed the number she'd been given countless times over the past several weeks, always with the same results. Not a single one of the messages she'd left had produced results. At first she'd been too distracted to wonder about it, but now she was beginning to be seriously concerned. If Miss Mitty was ill, it might explain why she had suddenly announced her retirement and moved to Georgia to be close to a newly widowed niece. She hadn't wanted anyone to worry about her.

Come to think of it, Miss Mitty had never really trusted Will Jordan. As a rule, people whom she didn't trust rarely remained at BFC very long. Jordan was an exception. If Mitty Stoddard didn't trust a person there was usually a sound reason, even if it wasn't apparent at the time. Val was sure she had voiced her reservations where it would do the most good, but for once in their long association, Frank Bonnard must have disagreed with her.

Val sighed. She desperately needed someone to bounce her ideas off, and Miss Mitty would be perfect. Under all that lavender hair lurked a surprisingly keen mind. Darn it, it wasn't like her not to return a call. The last thing she'd said before boarding the plane to Atlanta when Val had driven her to the airport was, "You call me now, you hear? You know how I feel about your young man." Val had been engaged at the time. "But then, you won't listen to an old woman. I guess I can't blame you." She'd laughed, wattles swaying above the navy suit and lacy white blouse with the tiny gold bar pin fastening the high collar. "Once you set the date, you let me know and I'll make plans to come back. Belinda and Charlie are getting along in years—the last thing they need is a big, fancy wedding."

Belinda was two years younger than Mitty Stoddard, and no one knew Charlie's exact age. As it turned out, Miss Mitty had been absolutely right about Tripp Ailes, but that wasn't the reason Val was so desperate to get in touch with her now. Was she even aware of all that had happened since she'd moved to Georgia? The collapse of BFC had been big news in the northeast for a few weeks—the *Wall Street Journal* had covered it, with updates for the first week or so. But it had probably been worth only a few lines in the business section of the *Atlanta Constitution*, or whatever newspaper Miss Mitty read now.

She would keep on trying, but in the meantime she had work to do before she could settle down with those blasted files. If there was a method in her father's filing system, she had yet to discover it. Brilliant, Frank Bonnard had undoubtedly been; organized, he was not.

Absently, she scratched her chin, leaving another smear of dirt. After waiting this long, the files could wait another day or two. She was making inroads on years of dirt and neglect—the pungent aroma of pine cleanser now replaced other less-pleasant smells, but it was still a far cry from the fragrance of gingerbread and Cape jasmine she remembered from so long ago.

"Up and at 'em, lady."

She didn't budge from the chair. She could think of several things she'd rather be doing than scrubbing down another wall. Shagging golf balls barefoot in a bed of snake-infested poison ivy, for instance.

Okay, so she was procrastinating. Scowling at the heap of filthy paper towels on the floor, she admitted that sooner or later the house would be as clean as she could get it and then—*then*—she would focus all her attention on going through her father's files with a fine-tooth comb.

Not even to herself would Val admit the smallest possibility of finding evidence of her father's guilt.

Three

A few hours later, with both the furniture and the downstairs windows sparkling—on the inside, at least—Val collapsed onto one of the freshly scrubbed kitchen chairs. She kicked off her Cole Haans and sipped on a glass of chilled vegetable juice, hoping that that and peanut butter constituted a balanced diet.

The ugly green refrigerator probably dated from the sixties. It was noisy and showing signs of rust, but at least it was now clean, inside and out. And if it wasn't exactly energy efficient, neither was she at the moment.

Marian had relayed the promise that her phone would be hooked up sometime today, which was a big relief. New number equaled no crank calls. She'd had to go outside and stand near the road to get even an erratic signal on her cell phone. After today, though, she could hook up her laptop, deal with her e-mail and check out the Greenwich newspapers to see if there'd been any new developments since she'd left town.

That done, she'd better start composing a résumé. Unfortunately, the only kind of work in which she had any experience was the kind that paid off more in satisfaction than in wages.

"Ha. How the mighty have fallen," she said, dolefully amused.

How much would a private investigator charge to dig into her father's records? The same records that had been turned inside out by swarms of experts?

Too much, probably. Anything was too much, given her present circumstances. Besides, even if she could have afforded to hire an investigator, she wasn't sure she could trust him with her father's personal files. Was there some code of ethics that said a private investigator had to turn over any incriminating evidence he might find?

"Dad, I'm out of my element here, you're going to have to give me a hint," she whispered now. Will Jordan might be still under investigation, but Val had a feeling he was going to find some way to pin the whole thing on Frank Bonnard. Why not? Her poor father was in no position to defend himself.

Val was feeling more inadequate with every day that passed. If she got lucky and found evidence that would vindicate her father, then she could be charged with concealing that same evidence. Couldn't win for losing. Classic case, she thought ruefully.

Finishing the last of her vegetable juice, she wiped her watering eyes with a grimy fist and went to see who had just pulled into the front yard. Marian had mentioned stopping by later today on her way to pick up her daughter at preschool. Still blinking, Val peered through the newly cleaned glass panel beside the front door. Or maybe it was the phone people.

It wasn't Marian. The vehicle that had just pulled up behind her own didn't look like any telephone van she'd ever seen. It wasn't even a van, it was a junker—a collection of mismatched parts. As for the driver...

Did she know him? There was something vaguely familiar about that thick, sun-streaked hair, the angular features—the wide shoulders that threatened the seams of his navy windbreaker. Her gaze moved down past the narrow hips to a pair of long legs that looked powerful even under loose-fitting jeans. He was definitely what her friends called a hottie. And the rush of sudden warmth she felt sure wasn't coming from that creaking old oil heater.

He stopped beside the sprawling palmetto that fanned out to cover the for rent sign she'd forgotten to take down. Bracing his legs, he shaded his eyes against the harsh sun and surveyed the front of her house. Not only was his face oddly familiar, but there was something about his stance—feet apart, one thumb hooked in the pocket of his jeans, that nudged the backside of her memory.

Could she have seen him somewhere? At the post office? The grocery store? She might've forgotten those rugged, irregular features, but that indefinable quality that was loosely referred to as sex appeal for want of a better word, would be hard for any woman to overlook. He had it doubled in spades, as the saying went.

Could she have met him before? She'd be the first to admit that her mind was stuffed with so many details, she had trouble remembering whether or not she'd even had breakfast this morning, much less what it had been.

Oh, well…peanut butter toast and hot tea, that was a given.

Still, even his vehicle looked vaguely familiar, and cars weren't her thing. She'd driven the one her father had given her for her twenty-sixth birthday until two weeks ago when she'd traded it in for something larger, older and a lot cheaper, plus a nice amount of cash.

On the other hand, how often did one see a rust-brown-and-primer-gray SUV that looked as if it had been pieced together from junkyard components? With yellow molded plastic seats, no less.

She stepped back from the panel of glass beside the door, unwilling to be caught staring if he came any closer. The last time she'd felt this fluttery sense of uncertainty she'd been fifteen years old. On a dare, she had asked a certain seventeen-year-old boy to a dance and nearly thrown up before he accepted.

He took his time looking the house over—the uneven shutters, the mended porch post, the ever-so-slightly sagging roofline—almost as if he were sizing up what it would take to fix it.

And then the light dawned. This must be the handyman Marian had promised to find. Of course! That would explain his interest in the house. He was mentally preparing an estimate.

The question now was whether or not she could afford him.

"I'm sure I can rent it for you once we get it fixed up," Marian had said. "There's a growing market for low-end housing." And Grax's old house was certainly that, as much as it pained Val to admit it. "The last couple rented it as a fixer-upper," the rental agent went on to say. "Trouble is, they didn't fix anything, so you're probably going to have to put some money into bringing it up to standard before I can advertise it again. Look, why don't I call around and see who I can find to do the minimum?"

Val had nodded, not knowing what else to say. Catch-22. She had to spend money she didn't have to make money she desperately needed.

His deck shoes made no sound on the porch. She swallowed hard. *I really can't afford you, but oh, how I need you.*

Want you?

"Don't even go there, woman," she muttered.

His jacket was open slightly, revealing a gray sweatshirt bearing the letters OD'S HO. Underneath the soft, loose-fitting clothing he looked solid as a slab of hardwood. Pecs, abs—from here she couldn't see the gluts, but she had no doubt they were every bit as splendid as the rest of the glorious package. Compared to this man, her ex-fiancé on his best day wasn't even a blip on the horizon.

Standing just inside the front door, she waited until he'd knocked twice before opening the door. "Yes?" She had the eyebrow lift down pat, having learned it at an early age from Charlie, who, she was convinced, had picked it up from watching "Masterpiece Theater."

"Miss Bonnard?"

For a moment she was startled that he knew who she was, but of course, Marian would have given him her name. Hopefully, she'd also told him that Val could afford only a minimum of basic repairs.

She nodded. It would have helped if he'd had a high-pitched nasal drawl. Instead, his voice was better than Belgian chocolate. "If you'll come around to the back, I can show you what needs doing first." Everything needed doing first. Mentally, she tried to prioritize what absolutely had to be done, whether or not she could afford it.

Instead of taking her implied suggestion that he go around outside, the tall stranger stepped through the door and glanced around curiously, making her aware all over again of the shabby, mismatched furniture and the boxes still waiting to be unpacked.

"Back this way, then. The shower, I think first of all. It barely trickles when I turn it on and then it takes forever to drain." She glanced over her shoulder as she led him down the hall. "You can do plumbing, can't you?"

"Nothing major, I'm not licensed, but maintenance, sure."

"Ms. Kuvarky might have told you, I'm considering renting the back bedroom separately." She hadn't been, not seriously, but with what she'd been spending lately on cleaning supplies, the slightest income would help. "So I'd rather start there if you don't mind."

After that, she decided, the hot-water heater and then the windows. Maybe the roof. Patching, not replacing. It hadn't rained since she'd been here, but she didn't relish the thought of waking up in a cold, wet bed, and she'd noticed a few suspicious stains on the ceiling.

"I'll have to get my tools."

"Oh, well…of course. I mean, it doesn't have to be done today, although…"

He nodded, pursing his lips.

Mesmerized, she stared at his mouth, then shook herself back to reality. The back end of the house was freezing. The back door didn't fit any closer than the front. She needed this man for practical purposes. The last thing she wanted to do was scare him off before he even agreed to take the job.

After a cursory glance at the ugly, closet-sized bath, he turned his attention to the tiny adjoining bedroom. Val studied the room objectively, trying to see it through the eyes of a stranger. That mattress definitely needed tossing, but at the moment she couldn't afford to replace it. The furniture was old, but hardly old enough to be called antique. Not that there was anything really wrong with it that a lick of paint and a little judicious sanding wouldn't remedy. Anyone with half a brain could figure out country chic.

She shook her head. Repairs first. Interior decorating later, if at all. "I can bring one of the spare heaters down from upstairs and put it back here while you work. Oh, by the way—do you know anything about space heaters?"

"I know they're probably not cost-effective, depending on the local power rates."

She sighed. "I was afraid of that. There's an oil heater in the front room, but it doesn't heat much beyond that. How on earth do you suppose people used to get by?"

"Furnaces have been around a long time. Aside from that, fireplaces, quilts." He grinned unexpectedly. It was as if the sun suddenly burst from behind a cloud. "Long johns."

She blinked and said, "Yes, well...there were two fireplaces originally, but they've both been boarded up. I'm not sure the mice haven't been chewing on the cords of some of the heaters, so you might take a look while you're here." She paused, tapping her lower lip with her fingers, wondering how much of him she could afford.

Stop it! Don't even think what you're thinking.

"How much?" he asked. His eyes were the color

of single malt whiskey, only not as warm. Noticeably cool, in fact.

"To, uh—to do the work? I guess that depends on what needs doing most and how long will it take. I don't even know your hourly rate." The fleeting expression that crossed his face was impossible to interpret. She didn't even try.

"I mean, how much rent are you asking? What kind of terms?" he said.

If there'd been a chair close, Val would have dropped down on it. As there was only a three-legged stool, a sagging iron-framed bed and an oak dresser, she leaned against the doorframe and stared at him, her mouth open like a guppy waiting to be fed. "The, uh—the going rate, I suppose."

Whatever the going rate was. It probably varied wildly in different parts of the country.

"Kitchen privileges?"

God, yes. If the man could cook, she might consider paying *him*. She couldn't afford many more restaurant meals, and she was growing tired of peanut butter three times a day.

She assumed an air of competence she was far from feeling and hoped he bought it. "That's negotiable," she said coolly.

He nodded, gave the place one last look, then turned and headed down the hall toward the front door.

"You're leaving?" She hurried after him, wanting to plead with him to stay, but for all the wrong reasons.

"Tools. Be back in an hour."

Tools. Right. "What about…that is, how much—?"

At the door, he glanced over his shoulder. "A week's rent in exchange for fixing the plumbing and seeing to any other minor repairs."

She followed him outside. "Does that include doing something to my water heater and checking to see if the roof leaks?" she called after him.

Instead of answering, he lifted a hand, swung up into the driver's seat and swerved out onto the narrow blacktop called Back Road.

She stood there for several minutes, arms wrapped around her body for warmth, and wondered what had just happened. Had she really hired herself a handyman? Had she actually rented out her back room?

Had her fairy godmother touched her with a wand and produced…

Well, hardly Prince Charming, but maybe someone even better?

And yes, his gluts were every bit as good as the rest of him, she couldn't help but notice as he'd strode across her front yard.

Too keyed up to go back to work, Val considered the possibility that her renter-repairman might not be back. She hadn't even asked his name, and now she was too embarrassed to take her cell phone out to the edge of the road to call Marian and admit that she'd hired the man without even asking that much.

Where was her brain? You'd think she had never screened a single applicant or volunteer. That was part of her job—to keep troublemakers from worming their way inside and causing trouble. Activists. These days, for every worthwhile cause, there was almost always some group of malcontents with a different agenda.

This time she didn't have a cause, at least none that anyone else could know about. When and if he came back she would have him sign an agreement spelling out the terms of...whatever. Rent versus work with a possible sidebar on kitchen privileges. While she was at it she would also ask for references. If there were rules covering renters and rentees, they probably differed down here. Just about everything else did. Imagine having to drive to the post office to collect your mail.

Welcome to the real world, chicky.

That was what Tripp, her ex-fiancé, used to call her. Chicky. She'd hated it. He'd known it, which probably was why he'd done it. He'd loved to ruffle her feathers. The harder he tried, the more determined she'd been not to be ruffled. It was a game they'd played, one she had never particularly enjoyed.

Shivering, she backed up to the oil heater. She almost wished he could see her now, in all her grime. Pondering the possibility of adding another layer over her silk undershirt, her cashmere pullover and the boiled wool cardigan, she thought longingly of a deep, hot soak, with a handful of whiteflower bath salts. And as long as she was wishing, she might as well have a Sibelius symphony playing softly in the background, a warm toddy within easy reach and towels staying warm on a heated towel rack.

Dismissing the wishful dream, she collected a stack of change-of-address cards, located her pen, her address book and a roll of stamps, then settled at the coffee table. This was one task she could do herself and cross it off her list. Trouble was, the to-do list was growing faster than she could do.

The first name in her address book elicited a grimace. Ailes, Timothy III, other wise known as Tripp. Amherst, Yale law, junior partner in his father's law firm at age thirty-two. All-around jerk who had given her a two-carat engagement ring six months ago and asked for it back less than a week after the scandal broke.

"Sorry, chicky-poo." She scratched through the name and went on to the next entry.

No point in letting her dentist know where she was, she would hardly be seeing him again anytime soon. Fortunately she'd already had her teeth braced and bleached.

Her three closest friends—tennis partners, bridge partners and confidantes Felicity, Sandy and Melanie, had avoided her after the scandal broke. As stunned as she'd been by all that had happened, including her father's death, that had hurt her terribly. By the time they'd made the first overture it was too late. Numb with grief and still in shock, she had never returned their phone calls.

Now she addressed a card to each woman. They could respond or not, it no longer mattered. It was highly unlikely that they'd ever again be moving in the same circles.

"And you know what?" she murmured, staring at the out-of-date lighthouse calendar hanging crookedly on the far wall. "I don't even care any longer."

She made it all the way through the Ms before setting aside the stack and wandering into the kitchen in search of something edible. The choices were peanut butter or cheese and salsa on whole wheat.

She *had* to find work soon. Starving wasn't an option, and she didn't know how to beg. Not on her own behalf, at least.

He wasn't coming back. He'd said he was going to get his tools, but how far did he have to go?

Outside the hardware store, Mac tossed the newly purchased hand tools into the back of the Land Cruiser, considered picking up a sub before heading back and decided against it. He could grab something to eat after he'd checked out of the motel and moved into the fox's den.

Talk about luck. He'd figured on engineering an accidental meeting in a day or so, working his way into La Bonnard's confidence and picking up any crumbs of information she might let slip before applying the thumbscrews.

Something told him he might be in for a few surprises. The lady wasn't quite what he'd expected. Either that or she was a damned fine actress. Recalling the first time he'd heard her voice, he'd nearly laughed aloud this time when she'd tried to send him around to the back door. By all means, let's not forget our respective places.

With any luck, hers was about to change. The last time he'd spoken to him, his stepbrother had blamed the lack of progress on a combination of local politics, ego, ineptitude and territorial interests, which made for a pretty unsavory stew. Mac wasn't quite sure yet where Ms. Bonnard fit in, but she was definitely a player. Had to be. The lack of makeup and the smear of dirt on her face had thrown him for a minute, but once he was out of range, cool logic had kicked in.

The last time he'd seen her—the day he'd delivered Will's sunglasses—she'd been wearing white linen pants, a navy shirt and a green linen blazer. Her hair had been twisted into one of those classy-looking bundles on the back of her head, with tortoise-shell chopsticks sticking out the sides.

Today's version—grimy face and hair that hadn't recently seen a brush—took some getting used to. Always open to a fresh challenge, Mac told himself there was much to be learned here, starting with why the heiress-apparent was living in a dump instead of soaking up sunshine and umbrella drinks in some fancy resort. Best guess—she was playing it smart in case anyone bothered to track her down. While she hadn't advertised her plans, she'd made no real effort to cover her tracks.

He hadn't expected to get his foot in the door so quickly, but when he'd gone to check out the house and seen the for rent sign, a plan had started coming together. The handyman gig was a bonus, although he'd have to come up with a few answers when the guy she'd been expecting showed up. With any luck he'd see him coming in time to head him off.

This time he entered the house through the back door and called out to let her know he was back.

"Oh, good," she said, hurrying down the short hall with a wad of paper towels in her hand. Her version of work clothes reminded him of a fashion spread he'd seen recently in the Sunday supplement. "I was afraid you'd changed your mind. Before you get started, could I get you to help me pull out the refrigerator?"

She'd been grubby enough when he'd left to go buy tools—duplicates, for the most part, of tools he'd left back in Mystic. Now she was flat-out filthy. When his glance moved to her hair, she reached up and brushed it back from her face. The thick, shaggy braid was coming unraveled, a few stray tendrils curling around her high cheekbones.

"The fridge? Sure. After that, I'll get started on your shower." He wasn't exactly implying that she needed a bath, but it was about as close as he cared to venture. She should have smelled of dirt, sweat and stale grease. Instead he caught a whiff of something fresh and spicy that reminded him of warm nights in the tropics.

He walked the refrigerator out from the wall, something that obviously hadn't been done for the past few decades. Leaning past him to peer behind it, she shuddered. Then she said, "The phone man came while you were gone. That is, if you need to make any calls. Of course, long distance…''

''Cell phone,'' he said, and smiled. He'd wanted her a bit off balance, but damned if she wasn't teetering like a one-legged tightrope walker. If he didn't watch it, he might even start feeling sorry for her.

''Yours works?'' she said plaintively. ''I have to take mine nearly out to the road to get a signal, and even then it's iffy.''

Leaving her placing calls, giving out her newly acquired phone number, he headed toward the back of the house, whistling tunelessly under his breath.

Four

From the waist down, he was scrumptious, Val mused, gazing up at the man on the ladder, his upper torso disappearing through the trap door. And if that was a sexist observation, he could sue her. Not that she would dare voice the sentiment aloud, but a woman would have to be both blind and neutered not to notice. They'd been working together for a day and a half now. Actually, not always together, but in the same small house there was no way she could ignore the man. For one thing, he was usually tapping, hammering or scraping. Not only that, but he whistled while he worked. Did he have any idea how far off-key he was? Either he was truly tone deaf or he was going out of his way to get under her skin. But why would he do that?

As a plumber and a carpenter, he admitted to being adequate. When it came to inspecting the house wiring, he'd advised her to hire a licensed electrician. He had, however, checked the small heaters and the kitchen appliances, assuring her that the mice hadn't done any serious damage.

She'd asked him to check the attic for mice because of the scratching noises she still heard at night, and for leaks because of the suspicious circles on the upstairs ceiling. Only because it was rickety and she didn't want him breaking his neck and then blaming her faulty equipment had she insisted on steadying the ladder. The last thing she needed was a lawsuit.

As it turned out, there were squirrels in the attic, not mice. "I'll get some hardware cloth and nail it over the places where they've chewed through," he called down.

Hardware *cloth?* She hardly thought cloth would suffice, but she was already learning to trust his judgment. He'd been here what—two days? A day and a half? With no particular routine and no appointments, it was easy to lose track.

An hour ago she'd stepped out onto the porch to turn down her empty scrub bucket to drain just as he was crawling out from under the house, where he'd gone to see if the floor had rotted through behind her leaky washing machine.

"Defies all common sense," he'd said, backing out and dusting off his hands and knees. She'd swallowed hard and tried to erase the vision of that trim, muscular behind emerging from under her house.

"It does?"

"These days beach houses have to be anchored against wind, tides and all other acts of God. Law requires it. This place was obviously built before building codes were invented. It's been sitting on top of a few skinny piers for how long—sixty or a hundred years?"

"Who knows? But then, it's not on the beach," she said, pleased that the man took his work so seriously.

"Doesn't matter, inspectors are real persnickety about things like tie-downs and distance above sea-level."

"Persnickety. Is that a technical term?"

Grinning, he'd wiped his hands on a red bandana. "About as technical as we professional handymen get. Did you know a couple of your girders came from a shipwreck? I'd make it mid-nineteenth century."

Oh, great. She wasn't entirely sure what a girder was, but the last thing she needed was to have some historical group tying her up in legal knots so that she couldn't even rent out a room without an act of congress. "My great-grandmother probably inherited the house from her husband. Or maybe her father, I don't know."

"Pretty common practice in places like this, making do with whatever materials wash ashore." Wintery sunlight had highlighted his features. She'd stared, distracted, until he'd said, "No signs of termites so far as I can tell, but you might want to call in an expert. Floor under the washer's in trouble, though.''

''A new floor *and* an exterminator?'' Worried about the escalating costs, she'd asked how much of the floor needed replacing.

''No more than a square yard, probably. Let me look around in your shed, might be something there I can use, since it won't show. Or we could check out the beach if you'd rather.'' He had a quick grin that came more frequently now, but never lasted more than a few seconds. All day she'd found herself watching for it, deliberately trying to tempt it into the open again.

''Check the shed first,'' she said, wondering what replacing part of a floor would cost if she had to buy new material. That had been when he'd found the ladder. He had also found several pieces of scrap lumber and crawled back under the house again with a folding rule.

Lord, he was something, she thought now. With the weight of all she had yet to do resting squarely on her shoulders, she could still admire a splendid specimen of masculinity. Just went to show what a powerful force survival of the species could be.

Not that there was anything like that at play here, she assured herself, watching him descend the shaky ladder. She might need to buy a new one before he went up onto the roof.

''I'm just glad you managed to fix my water heater so I can soak my bones in a deep, hot bath tonight instead of making do with four inches of lukewarm water,'' she said as he folded up the ladder.

It occurred to her that after crawling around under her house and in her attic, he might have a few aching muscles of his own. Should she offer him a soak in her bathtub?

Get a grip, Bonnard, you don't have time to play Lady Chatterly even if your gamekeeper happens to be willing.

"Looks pretty sound up there," he said, nodding to the trap door. "I spotted a few possible leaks, mostly around the chimney. Probably needs new flashing. I can give it a go if you'd like, or you can call in an expert."

"No, you."

He nodded. He was still working for room and, as it turned out, board. Late yesterday afternoon they'd shopped for groceries together and split the bill. Mac had done the cooking and she'd cleaned up afterward. It was the perfect solution, so far as she was concerned. She had to eat, and her culinary talents began and ended with making toast and brewing a perfect pot of tea. At the moment she had to settle for tea bags, as she didn't even own a teapot.

Last night's dinner had been an enormous chopped steak doused with soy sauce and salsa, along with a plain boiled potato and bagged salad. Hardly gourmet fare, but she couldn't remember enjoying a meal more in ages. If that was an example of what she had to look forward to, she would definitely keep him.

Mac had mentioned buying a microwave and she'd told him if he wanted one, to feel free, but she wasn't yet ready to invest in any kitchen appliances. Her already meager budget was shrinking at an alarming rate—not that she'd bothered to tell him that. Probably didn't have to.

She'd checked the two regional newspapers for jobs, and even looked over the post office bulletin board. Jazzercise classes, a missing Jack Russell terrier and tax service. No help wanted ads. If nothing better turned up by the end of the week, she might have to take Marian up on her joking offer of a job cleaning cottages. By then, she should be well qualified.

Mac called the hardware store on her newly installed phone and discussed flashing material while she washed up for a late lunch. How much, she wondered, did flashing cost? She wasn't even sure what it was. Something copper? Copper was flashy. She suspected it was also expensive. The roof on her father's house was slate, the gutters solid copper, the best money could buy, Charlie had once boasted.

Amazing, the things she'd taken for granted. Leak-free roofs. Limitless hot water. Warmth.

"I'll replace the bulb in the front-porch fixture and clean out the gutters before I put the ladder away," Mac said, hanging up the phone.

"Can't it wait?" If he started in on another project, she would feel obligated to tackle one, too. She still had two rooms upstairs to go, but there was no pressing hurry. One of them wasn't even furnished.

"Might as well do it while I'm thinking about it. Or if there's something else you'd rather I start on, the gutters can wait until I do the flashing."

Distracted, she tried to think of her to-do list while her gaze moved over his backside. He was washing his hands at the sink, his sleeves shoved up over his tanned, muscular forearms. So far as she could tell, he wore a single layer of clothing above the belt. She was wearing three. Her layers concealed a bosom hardly worthy of the name, while his stretched to accommodate a pair of magnificent shoulders. Just from watching what he'd done so far, she was beginning to understand how a handyman might develop a set of muscles that would make a professional athlete envious.

"I don't suppose a few more days will matter," she said.

"No rain in the immediate forecast, I checked. Chilly, though. Lows in the high twenties, highs in the low forties."

It occurred to her that back home, forties wouldn't even be considered cold this time of year. Either the cold down here was different or she was growing more sensitive.

While he dried his hands on the fluffy, white-on-white monogrammed towel, she put on a kettle to heat for tea. The water had a slightly brownish tint, but no discernible taste. If it had been unsafe, Marian would have warned her.

She jotted down bottled water on her shopping list, then crossed it off. She seriously doubted if Grax had made her iced tea with Evian. Determined not to be distracted, either by the drafts leaking in around the windows or her moderately attractive handyman, she got out the box of Earl Grey teabags and two cups.

Moderately. Right. Like a blowtorch was moderately hot.

Lunch was sandwiches. She spread her own. Mac raised his eyebrows when she set the cup of tea before him. She should have asked what he wanted to drink instead of assuming.

"Here's sugar if you want it," she said, indicating the old-fashioned sugar bowl she'd found on a top shelf, which she'd like to think had belonged to her great-grandmother.

"No, it's fine as is, thanks." His expression said otherwise.

Her ex-fiancé, whom she was determined to forget, had thought nothing of sending a bottle of wine back if it didn't quite meet his expectations. She'd seen more than one sommelier roll his eyes when Tripp had held up an imperious finger.

What on earth had she ever seen in the man? Other than his George Clooney looks, his killer backhand, his low golf handicap and his flawless social skills?

Although not so flawless, as it turned out. Not in her book, at least.

Reaching for the last half of her sandwich, she caught sight of the square, capable hand that was resting on the table and wondered idly if Mac ever played tennis. Actually, she wondered a lot more than that.

Which reminded her that she'd never gotten around to asking for references. Marian would never have sent him around if he weren't to be trusted— still, she wondered about his background. The sweat- shirt he wore said WOOD'S HOLE, not OD'S HO. But then, anyone could buy a sweatshirt. Felicity had one that said Souvenir of Folsom Prison.

"You planning on living here permanently?" he asked.

She blinked at the question. Had he read her mind?

She hadn't thought beyond the immediate future, which included doing the detective work the inves- tigators weren't doing because they were convinced they'd already caught their man, even if they hadn't yet recovered the missing funds.

"I'm not sure…" Glancing around at the drafty old kitchen, she remembered the first time she'd ever seen it. From a child's point of view, it had all been an adventure. The island, the old house—the ship model and decoys that Grax had said her husband had made. My great-grandfather, Val thought now, marveling that she'd never even been curious about her ancestors. Grandparents were family, but great- grandparents qualified as ancestors. She had never really known any of her extended family.

Centered on the mantel she remembered the brass Seth Thomas clock that struck ship's bells instead of the hour. Grax had been explaining to Val why it struck eight times in the middle of the afternoon when her mother had insisted they really must leave if they were to catch the ferry to Ocracoke in time to catch the ferry to Cedar Island in time to reach Hilton Head in time to claim their reservations.

"I think I mentioned that my great-grandmother left me this house," she said now. Hesitating, she added, "I only visited it once, and now..."

He nodded, almost as if he knew what she was trying to say.

She didn't even know what she'd been trying to say. That she was grateful for a place to go after losing her home? That she was ashamed of neglecting one of her few relatives?

She was, painfully so. But she wasn't about to admit it, much less explain her initial reason for coming here. Not that he'd even be interested.

Watching him sip his tea, which had grown cold, Val wondered again what he was doing here. His accent wasn't local. At least it wasn't native. Perhaps he had relatives on the island—relatives who might even have known her own.

Or not. One of the benefits she had recently discovered was anonymity. At least now when a stranger spoke to her, it was usually to ask if she weren't Miss Achsah's granddaughter, not to ask if she was Frank Bonnard's daughter, and if so, how soon could they expect to be reimbursed for their lost savings.

"I heard you'd moved down," several people had said. People who'd known Grax. Friendly people, not prying—simply trying to place her in their context.

"That's right. She left me her house, so I'm living there now," she always replied, increasingly proud of her legitimate link to the island. Roots might not have mattered to her mother, but Val was more than ready to reconnect. Her father had been an only son whose parents had been killed in an embassy bombing back in the eighties. There was nothing for her back in Greenwich, but here? Time would tell.

Mac finished his thick ham, cheese, lettuce, onion and salsa on rye and shoved his chair back. Slinging one leg across the other, he picked up his cup, stared blandly at the tepid brew and set it down again.

"More tea? I could heat more water." She half rose from her freshly scrubbed white-enameled chair.

"Thanks, I'm fine." He frowned. She had a feeling he had something on his mind and was searching for the best way to phrase it.

Please tell me you're not backing out of our deal, she thought anxiously. There was still the flashing and the floor under the washer. The washer itself, for that matter. The thing leaked, and she certainly couldn't afford to replace it.

Had he noticed the way she'd looked at him when he was on the ladder or backing out from under the house? Was he uncomfortable sharing a house with her? There was no way they could avoid close contact in such a small house. The least thing—reaching into the same kitchen cabinet at the same time so that their hands brushed, or playing dodge as they passed in the hallway, one carrying a basket of laundry, the other a handful of tools—took on added intimacy.

Once in the middle of the night, unable to sleep,

she'd padded into the kitchen for a glass of milk and he'd been there. In a chair that had been turned toward the window, he'd been seated with his back to her, yet he'd known she was there. He couldn't have heard her, yet he hadn't even had to turn around. Barefoot and bare-chested, he'd been wearing only a pair of sweatpants. "Can't sleep?" he'd asked, his voice edged with middle-of-the-night roughness.

"Thirsty," she'd mumbled, and that had been the end of it. She'd poured her milk, taken it back to the bedroom with her and forgotten to drink it. At least the focus of her worries shifted to something more pleasurable, if no more productive, than how to get to the bottom of what had happened back in Greenwich.

Neither of them had mentioned it the next day. He had to know women found him attractive. Thank goodness they were both sensible adults and not impressionable, impulsive, hormone-driven kids.

"Why don't we go in where it's warm before we tackle the next job?" he said. She'd mentioned being constantly cold, and the drafty kitchen was on the northeast side of the house, directly facing the wind.

Darn it, if he was going to be nice to her, all bets were off. Sex rarely tempted her, it was just something a man expected from any woman he dated more than once, especially if he gave her a ring. Personally, she could take it or leave it. Mostly, she'd rather leave it. Tripp had suggested she talk to her physician about hormone supplements before they were married.

There was definitely nothing wrong with her hormones—if nothing else she had learned that much over the past few days. Actually, what tempted her even more than the aura of sexuality Mac wore as casually as a favorite pair of faded jeans was the sense of strength he radiated. Not the macho-aggressive kind of strength, but the warm, benign kind. She found herself wanting to lean on him, to curl up in those powerful arms and forget everything but the moment.

Of course, if her hormones wanted to get in on the act, who was she to argue with nature?

Suddenly the small house felt entirely too intimate, almost as if it hummed with an energy all its own. "Can we get to the washing machine sometime today?" she asked abruptly. "I really do need it, but not if it's going to flood again and fall through the floor."

"I'll check out the hoses." To add to an already potent mix, he had one of those deep, quiet voices that registered in her nethermost regions.

"Thanks." Feeling a restless need to do something physical, she wandered into the living room, averting her face from the box of file folders that still awaited her attention.

He followed, lingering in the open doorway. It was toasty warm in the small room. If there'd been an open fire, she'd have avoided it like the plague, but there was nothing romantic about a smelly old oil stove.

She said, "I suppose now that the useable parts of

the house are as clean as they're likely to get anytime soon, I might as well finish unpacking." Two boxes remained, one of odds and ends, the other containing files. She'd already dipped into the latter several times, coming away after each session more frustrated, none the wiser.

"Need any help?"

"Oh—no, thanks. It's just..." She needed help, but she doubted if his talents ran to bookkeeping or accounting. Hers certainly fell lamentably short. From what she'd seen so far, most of the files should have been shredded months, even years ago. Old bank statements for people she'd never heard of. Other papers, none of which appeared to be related to BFC. Sooner or later she was going to have to wade through every single item in search of something she probably wouldn't recognize if she saw it.

Why, she kept asking herself, had her father asked her to remove these particular files from his study? Following his instructions, she had gathered up only the unlabeled ones, leaving the alphabetized ones in place.

Could she have got it wrong? She'd been frantic that day—she might have misunderstood.

God, she hated feeling so inadequate.

Sighing, she stared at the stove that had been finished to resemble wood grain, which suddenly struck her as absurd. Nerves tight as a bowstring, she snickered.

"Something funny?"

"The stove." She nodded toward the ugly metal

box that sat on a brown metal pad in front of the boarded-up fireplace. "Would you call that a pecan or a rosewood finish?"

Mac glanced at her, saw her blink away a film of moisture, but remained silent.

"These fumes," she grumbled. "What would it take to get rid of the stove and open up the fireplace again?"

"An adjustment in your insurance policy, for one thing," he said dryly. He sniffed. The fumes were barely noticeable. The lady was edgy. Too much pressure applied too fast, he cautioned himself, and she'd either clam up or break.

Somewhat to his surprise, he was no longer certain he wanted her to break. The more he was around her, the more unwelcome doubts were creeping in. Will had called late last night to ask if he'd learned anything yet.

"Look, you might as well know," his stepbrother had said. "Macy's left me. She said her lawyer would be in touch, so I guess it's official."

"Hey man, that's tough." What could he say? Congratulations?

"Yeah, like I really need another lawyer in my life."

Now Mac studied the woman who was backed up to the stove, toying with a place on her inner thumb where a blister had burst. "Don't pick at it," he warned. "Where's your first aid stuff? You need to put something on it."

"I forgot to bring any." A wistful smile flickered

past so quickly he thought he might've imagined it. She snagged her full lower lip between her teeth, shifting his attention away from her hands.

"Salt'll toughen your skin up, but it'll burn like the devil."

"No thanks, I'm healthy as a horse." This time the smile lingered long enough to knock the wind out of his sails.

"Why do you think there are veterinarians?"

She rolled her eyes. "I'd better get the rest of the plastic on the windows before I tackle the other rooms upstairs. I did my bedroom and the bathrooms first thing, but I keep the other rooms closed."

He could have told her that her makeshift storm windows wouldn't do her much good, with all the gaps she'd left between staples, but he didn't. Instead, he said, "Let me do the rest. I can reach without having to stand on anything." Meanwhile, the air leaks from those she'd already covered would serve to offset any fumes from the old stove.

Besides, he didn't want to see her balanced on one of those spindly kitchen chairs, her shapely little behind roughly at eye level. He remembered too well the legendary sirens that reportedly lured unwary seamen to their death.

"You never did say where you were from," Val ventured a few hours later as she dried the last dish and placed it in the cabinet. The dinnerware was mismatched, most of it cheap and ugly. There were only a few pieces of the delicate pattern she half remembered from her one and only visit.

"Hmm?" He was peering out the window at the traffic rolling past, mostly SUVs with rod holders affixed to one or the other bumper like big snaggled teeth.

Forthcoming, he wasn't, but as long as they were sharing a house, it only made sense to know something about him. She was beginning to suspect that he was no ordinary handyman. In fact, he occasionally struck her as almost scholarly. Not that a handyman couldn't be educated, but still...

An out-of-work professor? One on sabbatical? One who couldn't get tenure, perhaps, and had quit in a huff?

Whatever else he was, MacBride wasn't the huffy type.

"New England," he said. "Mostly coastal."

It took her a moment to remember what she'd asked him. That explained the shirt. "I'm from Connecticut, isn't that a coincidence? How long have you been here on Hatteras Island?" *In other words, what's a splendid creature like you doing clanking around in a tool belt in exchange for room and board?*

Something didn't add up, and she wanted it to. She really, really wanted him to be exactly who and what he professed to be. The last thing she needed was one more mystery to deal with.

"Not long," he said in answer to her inquiry.

"Me, either. Actually, I believe I mentioned that

I'd barely moved in when you came along. Thank goodness Marian found you—she was afraid all the available help was tied up on all these cottages under construction.''

The odd look that came over his face was gone too quickly to interpret. He shrugged and said, "Lucky I was between jobs."

"Lucky for me." But the more she was around him, the more certain she was that there was more to MacBride than met the eye. Not that what met the eye wasn't distracting enough.

They chatted a few more minutes while she wiped off the table and counters, comparing the New England coast with the mid-Atlantic area. Val picked over his brief responses, searching for clues. When Mac switched topics and mentioned the weather, she said, "It might be a good idea to check the oil in the tank if you know how. I'd hate to have to rely on those little space heaters."

"I'll check next time I go outside."

To think she had always taken heating and air-conditioning for granted. Considering how much her father had spent on her education, from boarding school through college, she couldn't help but think what a waste it had been. She could probably qualify as a candidate for one of those TV reality shows. Sheltered woman, loaded with social graces, falls out of the nest and gets smacked upside the head by real life.

Tripp used to talk about the "little people," as if a lower tax bracket were indicative of an entirely different species. It had always irritated her, but she'd let it pass. Tripp had political aspirations. He was going to be the "champion of the little people."

No wonder he'd been so quick to dump her, she thought, more amused than hurt. A business scandal that included not only a loss of wealth and social position, but a father-in-law who'd died in jail waiting to be indicted for embezzlement from his own company, was hardly the kind of baggage an ambitious young politician needed.

On the other hand, she was now one of the "little people" he'd vowed to help. Could he help her to learn to use a washing machine without flooding half the house? Or show her how to wield a mop and a broom without raising trophy-sized blisters on thumb and forefinger? Or cook bacon without setting off the smoke alarms?

She became aware that Mac was studying her with a curious look on his face. "What?" she snapped.

He flipped his hands palm up in a gesture of surrender. "You were looking pretty grim there for a minute."

"I was thinking about—about my furniture."

He nodded slowly, as if he might be evaluating her sanity.

"Well, you've got to admit it's ugly."

"I've seen better." And before she could comment, he added, "Seen worse, too. Hey, it's not so bad. At least it's comfortable...for the most part."

"All the same, I intend to replace a few things in

the very near future, starting with the mattresses and bedsprings.''

That is, if Marian still needed someone to clean cottages.

''Plywood's good enough for me. I'll do your bed, too, if you'd like. And by the way, you need new batteries in the smoke detectors. The one in the hall's started clicking.''

''Put it on the list.'' She wiped up a damp spot on the counter with more energy than the task demanded. ''I guess you'd better cook the bacon from now on. I probably wore it out. The smoke detector, not the bacon. Either that or stock up on batteries.''

He smiled and finally she did, too. His smiles were contagious and she was far from immune. It occurred to her that Miss Mitty would have liked him, and Mitty Stoddard's people-instincts were infallible.

Later that afternoon Val went through a file full of receipts for landscape services, plumbing and a new set of tires, most of them dated between two and eleven years ago.

Her father had scribbled across most of them—meaningless words, initials and series of numbers that defied interpretation.

''I need an aspirin,'' she muttered. ''Either that or a Rosetta Stone.''

Five

Tired of the fruitless task of searching for a needle in a paper haystack, Val headed for the kitchen for something rich and sinfully decadent. Lacking anything better, peanut butter dipped in chocolate syrup would serve as an antidote to frustration, only she didn't have any chocolate syrup.

Speaking of sinfully decadent, Mac was on his knees under the kitchen sink, an array of tools and a section of drainpipe beside him. She paused in the doorway to admire the view.

"Hmm?" he said, glancing over his shoulder.

"Nothing. That is, I thought we might take a peanut—that is, a tea break between chores."

He backed out, bumped his head on the edge of

the sink and started to swear, but cut it off. "Are we between chores?"

"I am. I've just gone through a dozen years of worthless receipts for a house I don't even own. I had no idea plumbers charged so much. Are we sure I can afford you?"

Sitting cross-legged on the floor, he grinned up at her. "Depends. How good you are with a pipe wrench?"

"About as good as I am with a frying pan."

"That good, huh?" He chuckled, and in one fluid movement, came to his feet only inches from where she was standing.

She inhaled sharply, aware of the intoxicating aroma of clean male sweat and the laundry detergent she'd bought because it promised sunshine-fresh results. "Yes, well…we all have our talents."

His eyes sparkled like polished amber. "Any in particular you'd care to brag about?"

She stepped back and tripped on a chair. He caught her arm before she could fall. "Let me guess," he said, briefly steadying her against his body. "You're a ballet dancer, right?"

No, she was a blithering idiot. She'd heard the term *brain drain,* but she'd never before experienced it personally. She backed away and he let her go, watching her as if he knew to the exact heartbeat how his touch affected her.

"How'd you guess?" When poise deserts, play the clown. "Three years, starting at age five." She struck a pose. "I was the one whose tights were always twisted, the one who was forever relegated to the back row because I was always two steps out of synch with the rest of the chorus.''

He laughed as he was meant to do and the moment passed, leaving her breathless, but otherwise unharmed. Now that she knew how susceptible she was, she'd take care to avoid further touching. Consider him her personal poison ivy.

"How about you? You're musical, right?" A little polite sarcasm couldn't hurt. "I've heard you whistling.''

"Ouch," he said softly. "That smarts. I'll have you know I played comb and tissue with a four-man band when I was in seventh grade. I wanted to be one of the Bee Gees. Never got the call, though."

"So you reluctantly settled for being a repairman," she said, and this time they both laughed. What had happened, she wondered, in the years between comb-and-tissue player and pipe-wrench wielder?

"Among other things. But about your plumbing," he said, a hint of laughter lingering in his eyes, his voice.

She really didn't want to hear about her plumbing, it was those "other things" she was curious about. "Let's go outside first, shall we? The front porch is sunny and out of the wind.'' And the kitchen was too darn small. The entire house was too small. For all she knew, the whole island might not be large enough for her to ignore his presence.

Avoiding the swing by mutual consent, they sat in

the weathered Adirondacs, feet propped on the rail. There was a small graveyard on the other side of the road, backed by acres of marsh and stunted maritime forest. Two white herons flapped lazily across the rushes to land on the pale branches of a bay tree.

The not-uncomfortable silence lasted several minutes. "I used to spend summer vacations at Mount Desert Island," she said thoughtfully. "For Thanksgiving we usually went to Hilton Head. Christmas was Captiva Island—occasionally, Bermuda."

She was usually good at this—putting people at ease, encouraging them to open up, to give her some idea of whether or not they were suited for whatever position they were applying for. Even among volunteers for charitable causes, there were troublemakers.

He nodded, but said nothing. She wondered where he usually vacationed...or if he did. Maybe this, for him, was a vacation. "My great-grandmother's buried over there," she said, indicating the small cemetery. "Probably more of my family, too." Aware of how that must sound, she said, "I mean, I never met either of my great-grandfathers. I wish I could have known them, but I didn't." Her gaze slid away, "For that matter, I never really knew my mother all that well," she admitted. Embarrassment washed over her. She *never* discussed personal matters with strangers. "Sorry. You were saying—? About my plumbing?"

Instead of rescuing her, he said thoughtfully, "I

don't know if it's possible for a child to know a parent—another family member. Not objectively, that is.''

''Is that MacBride the psychologist speaking? Or MacBride the philosopher?'' Before he could reply, she said, ''Let's stick to plumbing, shall we?'' Okay, so he knew how to dismember a drainpipe and she didn't. Big fat deal. That didn't mean she was inferior, it just meant that their talents lay in different areas. At least she could carry a tune. He couldn't find a C-sharp if he tripped over it. ''You were about to tell me what's wrong with it.''

So much for poise. Her face was on fire and she had no one to blame but herself. She couldn't remember feeling this embarrassed since she'd spilled a glass of wine in her date's lap and then tried to mop it up with a cocktail napkin.

''Well, for one thing,'' he said finally, ''your septic tank needs pumping.''

''My *what* needs pumping?'' One of her feet slipped off the railing.

''For another, your pipes are old and probably about to start leaking, if they don't already. Acid water eats away copper piping.''

It wasn't acid water that was eating holes in her composure. ''Great. I'm afraid to ask if there's anything more.''

''You'll probably need to replace them with PVC in a year or so.''

She glanced at the sky. No help there. Then she frowned at the once-white, size-seven sneaker that was still propped on the rail beside his putty-colored size-twelve Docksiders. "I'll make a note. Is that all?"

"You need a new well pump."

"A new *well pump?*" Her other foot plopped to the floor and she sat up straight.

"Hey, don't panic. Thing's probably good for another few months, at least. On the other hand, it could quit tomorrow. Leaky foot valve'd be my guess."

"A leaky foot valve," she echoed numbly, wondering how much it cost to replace foot valves. Feet valves? She started to suggest corn plasters, but then she might have erupted in a horrible cackle. She didn't even know this woman she was becoming. It couldn't be the salt air—she'd breathed plenty of that without ever losing her cool.

"Can't claim I haven't been warned," she said brightly, fighting depression. Mood swings were nothing new to her after the past few months, but the troughs seemed to be deepening and there were no corresponding highs.

Mac reached across the narrow space between the two chairs and covered her hand with his. Well...perhaps a few highs. His hands were warm. Hers were cold. He had square palms, long fingers, and despite the fact that he'd been grunging around under her sink, his nails were in far better shape than her own.

"Hey, it's no big deal," he commiserated.

Maybe to him it wasn't. To her, with no job, a

house that seemed to be falling apart around her ears—a project she was afraid to tackle but desperately needed to finish, and a man she could no more ignore than she could ignore a tsunami, *everything* was a big deal.

But then, he had no way of knowing that, and she wasn't about to tell him. Her problems were just that—her problems. Sliding her hand from under his, she rose and moved toward the door. "I'll be in the living room if you need a hand putting the sink drain back together," she said, and fled before she could embarrass herself further.

Once inside the door, she paused to draw a steadying breath. All right, so she'd brought up her marginally dysfunctional family. She'd heard far more personal matters discussed at cocktail parties. Whose spouse was cheating with whom—who had just had a vasectomy. Whose silicon was starting to slip.

The box of files was the first thing that caught her attention when she wandered into the living room. She could think of a hundred things she'd had to dispose of one way or another in order to make room for those, plus the barest essentials. The Venetian seascape that used to hang in the dining room. The chaise lounge in the morning room, where she used to curl up with one of Belinda's romance novels when she grew tired of reading sixteenth-century poets or essays on the creative traditions of folk cultures in Appalachia.

And the piano. Even if she'd hired a moving van or rented a trailer to bring it with her, there was no room for it here. Was there even a piano tuner on the island? Probably not. She remembered hearing her father pick out simple melodies, mostly old songs from the forties. She'd given him a CD collection of songs from that era for Christmas one year, but whether or not he'd ever played them, she didn't know. She'd been too busy doing her thing in Chicago and later, in New York.

Oh, darn it, she was *not* going to cry! Was there any emotion more worthless than self-pity?

Her standard antidote was to think about all the women who, faced with overwhelming odds, attacked life with both hands and came out on top, Miss Mitty being a prime example. She had never married; her only family was the niece in Georgia whom she hadn't seen in years, yet she'd managed to build a satisfying and productive life for herself.

And there was Grax, a widow whose only son had died young, whose only granddaughter had ignored her existence. According to everyone Val had met since she'd been here, practically the whole island— certainly the entire village of Buxton—had claimed Achsah Dozier as a friend. She'd gardened and gone to church and even taken a driver's course for seniors at the Fessenden Center the year before she'd died, though she'd no longer owned a car. There'd always been someone to drive her wherever she wanted to go. She might have lived alone, but she hadn't been alone.

Val could do worse than emulate two women who

had been independent long before women's independence became a *cause célèbre*.

On his way out the back door, Mac glanced at the empty boxes waiting to be taken to the recycling center by the dump. It wasn't the empties that interested him, it was the box of file folders she'd made no effort to hide, which might or might not mean there was nothing there to hide. So far he hadn't found anything incriminating in the ones he'd gone through. He wasn't comfortable doing it, but he'd skimmed through a few of the files while she was out, knowing even as he searched that the type of information he was looking for wouldn't be easy to recognize. Sixteenth-century shipwrecks were probably easier to trace than offshore bank accounts.

When it came to deciphering ancient shipping records and ships' logs he was in his element, but high finance was another matter. That took training in financial crimes or forensic auditing. When and if he found anything that looked like incriminating evidence he would have to turn it over to the proper authorities and hope it proved what he'd set out to prove.

The fact that he was increasingly attracted to his chief suspect didn't make him feel any better about sneaking around behind her back. He'd been forced to remind himself more than once that Val Bonnard wasn't the first crook who didn't look the part. Hell, if crooks always looked the part, fighting crime would be a cinch. So she was funny and sexy and a good sport about being so totally out of her element—that didn't necessarily mean she was innocent.

It also didn't mean she was guilty, he admitted reluctantly. The odds were slightly better than even, he told himself, that she'd holed up here waiting for the heat to die down. That once things cooled off, she would light out for the Caymans or wherever she'd stashed the money, and never look back.

Yeah, right. That's why she wore herself out scouring every square inch of her dilapidated old ruin. Great cover. It almost had him fooled. Almost.

Mac had talked to his stepbrother every night since he'd been on location. Last night he'd confessed that things weren't moving quite as fast as he'd hoped. "Look, we both know I came down here expecting to find our prime co-suspect living it up in a cozy twelve-bedroom beachfront cottage complete with swimming pool, maid service and personal chef," he'd admitted the night he'd moved in, after Val had gone upstairs. Just to be safe, he'd waited until she was asleep and then gone outside to place the call.

"I thought you said the place she inherited was a dump."

"Yeah, well…happens I was right about that, but dead wrong about everything else. According to local tax records, the property's worth around fifty grand, max. The house is a fixer-upper. I've got someone checking to see if there's any possible link between her and any of the developers operating in the area. So far, no hits."

''Stick with it, okay? She's the only hope I've got unless someone comes up pretty soon with a smoking gun.''

Which they both knew was hardly likely, as the hunt had slowed to a crawl for lack of fresh evidence.

From his own professional experience, Mac knew better than to go into any project with a closed mind. If he'd been diving on what was supposed to be an eighteenth-century galleon and suddenly discovered sonar gear or a fiberglass hull, he'd have known immediately he was way off base. He'd come down here expecting to find a sharp little cookie who had socked away a fortune without even raising a blip on the radar screen. Instead, he'd found a gorgeous, sexy, likable woman with dirt on her face, cobwebs in her hair, wearing designer jeans and a Cartier tank watch to scrub floors. It had shaken him up some. He'd had to back off before he could confront her again with an open mind, using the excuse of collecting his tools. Since then things had gotten worse instead of better. For a guy whose profession demanded objectivity, he was having some pretty serious problems.

The woman he'd seen that day at the country club wearing a haughty look and a rock the size of an ice-cube on her third finger, left hand, was nowhere in evidence. The watch, maybe—and her clothes. Those carefully faded jeans she'd been crawling around in hadn't come from Target, no matter how you pronounced it.

The first time he'd ever seen her, he'd summed

her up as post-debutante, Junior League, the whole ball of wax. Now that he was getting to know her— up close and personal, as the saying went—his earlier impression was turning out to be a hundred-and-eighty degrees off course.

"If she's pulling a scam, she's damned good at it," he'd told his stepbrother two nights ago.

"Yeah, well…women can fool you," Will had replied.

Mac had tactfully refrained from mentioning Macy. Nor had he mentioned the woman he'd briefly been engaged to a dozen or so years ago, who had dropped him in favor of someone rich and good-looking. As he fit neither category, he'd wished her luck and headed to the Azores feeling freer than he had in months.

Val scowled at the files, then lifted the only other box yet to be unpacked onto the coffee table. Okay, so she was procrastinating. Every file she'd looked though so far had left her more puzzled than before. If there was anything significant to be found, it must have been written in invisible ink. On the backs and even on the face of old bills, personal bank statements and obsolete brokerage statements, she'd found the usual scribbled phone numbers, initials and obscure notations. Having served as fund manager for a few large charities, Val knew the value of keeping clean, meticulous records. Evidently, for all his business degrees, her father had missed that lesson.

With a sigh, she turned to the box on the coffee

table and lifted out a figurine he'd given her after her first ballet recital, before they'd realized that her talents, if any, lay in a different direction. She had a good ear for music, but it didn't extend to her feet. They'd laughed about it since.

Now she unwrapped the china ballerina and she set it on the mantel. Framed photographs carefully wrapped in a scarf she'd purchased in Scotland emerged next. She took a moment to study the pictures of her parents, taken in the late fifties, shortly after they'd been married. Val had always likened them in her mind to Sean Connery and Greta Garbo. Her mother's beauty still reminded her of Garbo's cool elegance. Val hadn't seen Lola Bonnard, or whatever her current name was, in several years. They'd met for lunch once when Lola had stopped over in New York on her way from London to San Francisco. Gazing at the photos now, she whispered, "Hi, Mom. Hi, Dad. You'd never guess where I am now."

Next she pulled out a miniature oil she'd always loved. The larger paintings had all been sold to a dealer, but this one she'd held back. It could go where last year's lighthouse calendar still hung, even though it would be lost on the twelve-foot wall space. She'd have to find a few more things to balance it. Prints, probably…if she could even afford good original prints. If not, reproductions would have to do.

It occurred to her fleetingly that she was beginning to think long-term rather than short-term. She didn't care to dwell on it.

For nearly an hour she unpacked and found places for the mementos she'd brought with her, putting her own stamp on the old house. Meanwhile she listened for sounds that might indicate what Mac was doing. Not that he was obligated to work eight hours a day, but she had come to enjoy knowing he was nearby working on some project or another. At close range he affected her in an entirely different way, but out of sight he was…comfortable. Companionable. Much as she imagined a husband might be.

Bite your tongue, woman!

She'd do better to concentrate on having her septic tank pumped, her pipes replaced and whatever needed doing to her foot valve done. By whom, a plumber or a chiropodist? Horribly expensive, no doubt, either way.

Mac appeared in the doorway just as she lifted the last item from the box. A tube of brand new tennis balls. Why on earth had she packed anything so useless? She'd forgotten her racquet—it was still at the club, not that it mattered. "Anyone for tennis?" she asked facetiously.

Grinning, he shook his head. "Not my sport, sport. Looks like the weather's closing in sooner than I expected. We've just got time for a sunset walk on the beach."

"You're joking, right?"

"No, I'm not. You need a break. You've been holed up in here long enough."

Not long enough to regain her perspective, obviously. No sooner had he appeared in the doorway than she'd lost track of what she was supposed to be doing. Come to think of it, a brisk walk—maybe even a fast run—might be just what the doctor ordered, never mind that sharing a sunset walk with a man who could send her hormones into a wild tango with no more than a single glance might do more harm than good.

"Bundle up, it's colder than it looks."

Immediately, her thoughts flew to the old Yankee courtship custom of bundling. "Five minutes," she said, wondering if a few more layers of clothing would serve to insulate her against the man.

Hardly. He hadn't done a single thing to encourage her, it was her own wayward imagination that needed insulating.

Instead of driving his four-wheel-drive vehicle onto the beach, Mac turned off the highway, drove past the small airstrip, deserted but for a single red-and-white Cessna, and parked near a chained-off entrance to a National Park Service campground. The place was obviously closed for the season. "You can warm up by stepping over the chain," he said.

"I thought you said a beach walk. Is this legal? I mean, are we trespassing or anything?"

"I understand the locals walk here year-around. There's a couple of boardwalks to the beach. We'll take one over, walk the beach and take the other one back. Suit you?"

He pocketed the car key and nodded toward the chained entrance. The deserted campground was situated among a series of high wooded dunes and deep, jungle-like valleys. "This way," Mac said, steering her right when she would have turned left and headed up a steep incline.

He set a rapid pace and neither of them spoke for several minutes. She wore a white mohair stocking cap, but the wind found ways inside her anorak. "There's nobody here," she said, panting only slightly. "I thought you said the locals walked here."

"Way the weather's closing in, I guess any walkers have already given up and gone home."

"Sensible people," she panted. He was making no allowance for her shorter legs.

"Might be a few fishermen on the beach," he offered.

"Freezing their bait off." She cast an uneasy glance at the rapidly darkening sky. When they came to a boardwalk, he touched her arm and gestured with a nod. "Leads to the beach," he said, "Come on, we'll be out of the wind for a few minutes."

Walking single file, they traversed the narrow boardwalk between scrubby pines and stunted, vine-covered oaks. Deer tracks were plentiful. The place was growing on her. Whatever else it was—an eclectic mixture, neither ticky-tacky nor self-consciously quaint—she rather liked it.

Before they were halfway there, the spray was visible above the wind-sculpted dunes with their dark mantle of hardy vegetation. Mac led the way and Val trudged behind him, determined not to complain of the pace he'd set. Housework, she was discovering, was no substitute for regular aerobic exercise.

When the boardwalk ended, she puffed up the last steep stretch of slippery white sand. And there it was, wild as any New England seacoast, only different. Without the rocks, the surf lunged up onto the flat, sandy shore, leaving behind trails of creamy foam and dark seaweed. "Oh, my mercy," she whispered. "It's…magnificent."

And it was. Winslow Homer water beneath a darkening sky that was streaked with all the colors of a Turner palate. Overhead, so close she could see the yellow on their heads, a trio of pelicans followed the row of dunes, taking advantage of the air currents.

There wasn't a living soul in sight. No fishermen, not so much as a solitary beach walker. As if by magic, she could feel months of anxiety slide from her shoulders, leaving her oddly weightless. Lifting her face to the wind, she closed her eyes and inhaled deeply.

Mac remained silent but she could feel his presence. He was a part of it all, even though he was standing several feet below on the seaward side of the dunes. They might have been the only two people in the world. Feeling the cold, damp spray on her face, she licked her lips, savoring the bite of salt. Then, sensing his nearness, she opened her eyes.

Standing with his back to the wind, he captured one of her hands between his. Hers were gloved. His were bare. It struck her as funny—Lord knows why—and she laughed. He smiled. Moving closer so that his body shielded hers, he shifted his hand to her shoulder and laid a finger across her lips. Overhead, hundreds of birds streamed across the sky in chevron formation, like tiny black ants traversing a gray marble counter.

Mac tugged off her stocking cap and pointed skyward. *Listen,* he mouthed.

She listened.

And then she heard it, the whisper of hundreds of pairs of wings, audible even over the roar of the sea. The kind of awareness that came over her was like the chill she'd experienced once when she'd been touring abroad and she'd happened to find herself alone in the ruined chapel of an ancient monastery. Voices—echoes, whispering through time.

His face crinkled into a smile as they shared the brief magic moment. Sea oats whipped around her legs. Raw wind rocked her physically, bringing tears to her eyes. "I should have worn sunglasses," she murmured, embarrassed by the flood of unexpected emotions.

"Valerie?"

"What kind of birds were they? Not geese, I didn't hear a single honk. Ducks?"

"Cormorants," he said. And before she could think of something witty, or even appropriate to say, he kissed her.

Wrapped in the wind, surrounded by the mingled scent of salt and millions of tiny dead organisms washed ashore with the mounds of Sargasso weed, he rocked his mouth over hers, pressing gently until she opened for him. Nothing in her entire life had ever felt so inevitable. His arms, strong, warm and anything but safe, pressed her against him so tightly that layers of clothing seemed to fall away. She felt *him*. His essence—his heartbeat.

His erection.

From far away, a voice whispered, *You don't even know this man!*

Another voice, stronger, far more assured, whispered back, *Oh, yes I do. I've known him all my life, I just never knew where to find him.*

The kiss ended far too quickly. They were both breathing heavily when he finally lifted his head. He swallowed hard, shook his head as if dazed, and she waited for him to speak. To say something trivial, anything to anchor her in her shaky world again.

A drop of rain struck her face. In a gravelly voice, he said, "Come on, let's head back."

Six

They were less than halfway along the boardwalk when the rain struck in earnest. Mac might have grabbed her hand to pull her along, but there was no room on the narrow pathway, so he let her go ahead. When they were nearly at the end, he pointed to a park service facility nearby. Val didn't ask questions. By now she was breathless, laughing and freezing, her shoes and jeans soaked through.

The small facility was locked, but there was a covered porch separating the men's side from the women's. Leaning against the back wall she laughed until her sides ached.

"What's so funny?" Mac asked.

"I don't know. Nothing." He shot her a quizzical

look, and she said, "Didn't you ever laugh at nothing?"

"Not in the past twenty-odd years. Not while I was sober."

Her laughter died and she bit her lip, picturing a much younger John MacBride, a little bit drunk, a little bit vulnerable—not nearly so sure of himself. The stabbing pain she felt in the region of her heart had nothing to do with having run a fast quarter of a mile in the driving rain.

Who are you? she wondered.

"You're freezing," he said gruffly, and before she could protest he gathered her in his arms and stood with his back to the blowing rain, offering her what shelter he could provide.

It wasn't the cold that bothered her. Cold she could handle. What bothered her—frightened her—was the fact that she was wildly off balance, deeply in lust and trying hard to ignore the whisper of common sense that urged her to back off, to run—to forget everything except for the reason she had come here to the island. Her personal needs weren't important.

Her obligations were. "I'm not freezing," she said, inhaling the healthy male scent of his skin. "I'm—I'm hungry."

"Me, too." There was no mistaking his meaning. Not even the layers of clothing that separated them could disguise the fact that he was seriously aroused. Instead of remarking on it, or acting on it—not that there was any way they could under the circumstances, he said, "Tell you what. Once it slacks enough to get to the car, I'll drive you up the beach for a sub. There's a place in Avon.''

She didn't say a word. Instead, she burrowed her face in the warmth of his throat, clasped her hands around his back and savored the moment, knowing it wouldn't be repeated. She couldn't afford the distraction.

The rain ended as suddenly as it had begun. When he stepped back, she could have cried. Instead, she brushed past him and clambered down the steps. Once she got her directions straight, she marched out in front, setting a faster pace than was comfortable in clinging denim and soggy sneakers. With his longer legs, he had no trouble keeping up with her, even when she broke into a jog.

Wordlessly, Mac unlocked the Land Cruiser and she grabbed a handhold and swung herself up unaided. Neither of them spoke when he passed the turnoff onto Back Road and followed Highway 12 to the village of Avon, some six miles to the north.

Not a word, the entire six miles.

By the time Mac pulled up under the long-limbed live oak tree in the side yard and shut off the engine, he had more or less put things into perspective.

Okay, so he'd kissed her. He was thirty-seven years old. He'd lost track of the women he'd kissed, including the woman he'd nearly married. So what the hell difference did one more kiss make? It was no big deal.

She'd kissed him back, too. Sweet, hot and wet,

with cold noses pressed against cold cheeks. Sand whipping around their legs, rain blowing in on their backs while he tried to come up with some excuse to shed a few layers of clothing.

He needed his brain examined for even touching her. Ever since yesterday, or maybe the day before, when he'd walked into the kitchen and seen her with her head in the oven, her shapely little behind wriggling in harmony with her shoulders as she chipped away layers of volcanic ash, he'd been semi-hard. Not a comfortable condition for any man, especially one on a mission of entrapment.

If that weren't bad enough, he'd held the back door open a few minutes later when she'd headed outside with a box full of trash. After she'd sidled past him, her firm little butt pressing briefly against his groin, he'd had to go outside and whack weeds with a rusty scythe for half an hour before he was fit to come inside again.

At this rate he might need to invest in a suit of pikeman's armor, with the hinged steel apron.

"I ordered two twelve-inchers," he told her as he unlocked the front door. She'd opted to wait for him in the car when he'd gone inside to place their order. "You can have six inches tonight, and six tomorrow."

Ah, jeez, MacBride, cut it out!

"Onions?" It was the first time she'd spoken since he'd asked her what kind of sub she wanted.

She'd said, "Anything's fine."

Now he said, "Onions," and she said, "Cool."

The last thing he felt was cool, despite wet clothes, wet shoes and falling temperatures. He cut her a side-long glance and caught a glint of something like amusement flashing across her face, which he inter-preted as a good sign. Any expression at all was a good sign, even if it meant only, Might as well forget that damned kiss, buster. It never happened and it's sure as hell not going to happen again.

Of course, being a lady, she might not put it in exactly those terms, but the meaning was pretty clear. "You want a beer?" he asked once they got inside.

She was peeling off layers, one by one. Gloves, anorak, soggy stocking cap, sweater. He wondered if she was deliberately trying to be provocative. If she stripped all the way down to a G-string and a pair of pasties, he might take that as a sign of encourage-ment. Anything short of that, no way.

"House feels toasty, doesn't it?" she observed brightly.

The thermometer read sixty-two. "It won't for long," he said glumly. He switched on the heater.

She said, "Thank you," and offered to make tea.

He said, "No, thank you." They were rappelling off each other, neither of them willing to admit that their relationship, whatever it had been before, had undergone a change. "I bought a six-pack earlier to-day. Want one?"

She shook her head. He shrugged and opened a bottle for himself. Given a choice between Corona, one-percent milk or hot tea, he'd take beer every time. In moderation.

They ate in the living room, avoiding by mutual consent the closer confines of the kitchen. She settled in the middle of the sofa, ensuring that there wasn't quite enough room on either end for another passenger.

He dragged the heavy, fake-leather recliner over to the coffee table and sat across from her. While he unwrapped his meatball-with-all-the-extras, his peripheral vision took in her flushed cheeks and the way she avoided looking at him. The flush might be weather-related, but not the avoidance of eye contact.

Back to square one. Employer versus employee. Tenant versus landlady.

Hunter versus hunted.

They ate in silence until halfway through the meal when she asked how much she owed him for her supper. He started to swear but cut it off. "My treat," he said. "Next time you can pick up the check."

"Then thank you. It's very good."

He was tempted to laugh, damned if he wasn't. Whether or not she was ready to admit it, she'd been as turned on by that hot, sweet-salty kiss as he was, otherwise she wouldn't be sitting there like Lady Whatsername at a tea party. It occurred to him that he might have set his mission back a few days.

Or maybe not. Maybe now that he'd defused this crazy physical attraction he could concentrate on doing what he'd come down here to do.

Okay, so there was still some electricity sizzling between them. Roughly enough to light up Shea Stadium. It might help if he could take her to bed and make love until he was cross-eyed, but that wasn't going to happen.

It might also help if he could find whatever he was looking for and get the hell out—put a few hundred miles between them—but somewhere along the line, the idea had lost its appeal.

The rain droned on, accompanied by loud claps of thunder and brilliant flashes of lightning as the storm swept out to sea. Mac awoke with a throbbing head, signaling that a front had passed through during the night. Great, he thought, disgusted. Just what he needed to help him concentrate.

He switched on the shower, adjusted it to a few degrees below parboil and allowed it to beat down on the back of his neck. By the time he dried off and pulled on a pair of jeans and an old Columbia U. sweatshirt, the pain had settled like a ground-hugging fog. He could function, but by no means at peak efficiency.

After a pint of coffee and a bagel smeared with peanut butter, he headed upstairs to take apart and clean the trap under the upstairs lavatory. Val had mentioned that it took forever to drain.

She was nowhere in evidence. Her car was missing, too. Not that he expected her to check with him before leaving the house, but she might have done him the courtesy of leaving him a note.

He bumped his head on the porcelain bowl, swore and reached for a bucket to catch the sludge. From the looks of it, the thing hadn't been cleaned out since the Carter administration.

Where the devil was she, anyway? It was too early for the mail. So far as he knew, they weren't out of anything.

Once he'd reconnected the drain, he cleaned up the site and went in search of a screwdriver, a bit of sandpaper and a tube of graphite. The front-door lock was getting almost too stiff to key. Might as well finish up as many small jobs as possible in case he needed to take off in a hurry.

Her car was still missing when he glanced outside. It occurred to him that instead of cleaning the lock, he should be going through those damned files. He was half tempted to tell her the truth and ask for complete access, including whatever was on the laptop she had yet to unpack. Just because the captain had gone down with the ship, he could argue, there was no reason to take his second in command down with him.

It was that kiss that had messed up his mind, he told himself as he wiped graphite from his hands. Major mistake, in more ways than one. There'd been a growing tension between them even before that— sexual awareness didn't wait for an invitation—but at least before he'd kissed her she'd trusted him not to take advantage of the situation.

Now she was wary for all the wrong reasons. He didn't know which was worse: feeling guilty because she trusted him when, once he found what he was looking for, it might lead to her being arrested for concealing evidence, or feeling guilty because he was tempted to walk away and let Will handle his own case. Let his lawyer earn his pay for a change.

It was eating on him. Last night he'd had to take a couple of antacid tablets before he could get to sleep. Could've been the meatball sub, but chances were it was this growing conflict between his brain and his libido, between what he'd come down here to do and what he really wanted to do.

He was out in the kitchen trying to scrub the gray film off his hands when she pulled into the front yard. A minute later she stuck her head in the doorway and said, "Hi. Did I get any calls while I was out?"

Okay, so they were back to the old footing. Cheerful, but casual housemates. He could live with that. "No calls, sorry."

She sighed, and he wondered whom she'd been hoping to hear from. Unless it was a Swiss banker or a big development outfit it was none of his business.

By the time he put away his tools and reheated the coffee, which by now was roughly the consistency of crude oil, just the way he liked it, she was curled up in the recliner, rattling papers and humming something slow and bluesy. Hell, even her hum was sexy.

He'd give his new Viking drysuit to know what she'd found that put her in such a good mood. He had a feeling that if it was good for Bonnard, it was probably bad for Will.

* * *

Across the hall in the living room, Val unfolded the Home Depot flyer, scanned it quickly and laid it aside. Maybe later she could afford to get into remodeling. She had a few ideas, but neither the time nor the money to carry them out. Besides, she had too many things on her mind.

What on earth was she going to do about MacBride?

She knew what she wanted to do, but it wasn't going to happen. Even if he happened to be interested, she didn't have time for an affair. Not even a single session of mind-boggling sex. And she had a feeling it would definitely be that. She was hardly inexperienced, but mind-boggling didn't come close to describing her relationship with Tripp. Or even with the tennis pro she had briefly fallen in love with the year she'd graduated from college.

One thing about it—before she indulged in any sex at all, mind-boggling or otherwise, she would have to do something about that mattress. Which meant she was thinking about it.

Which also meant she needed to find out if Marian had been serious about that job offer. She'd gone out early this morning to ask about it only to find a sign on the door of Seaview Realty saying, ''Back at 1:00 p.m.''

Disappointed, she'd driven on to Conner's and picked up another can of oven cleaner and some industrial-strength hand lotion. From there she'd gone to the post office to mail the last of her change-of-address cards. Shoving them through the out-of-town slot, she'd wondered who among her closest friends—if any—would be the first to attempt a bit of fence-mending.

Hopeful, but not really expecting a letter, she'd opened her mailbox and found it crammed full of catalogs and flyers. Disappointed that that's all there was, she'd stopped short of dropping them into the recycling barrel. Even junk mail was better than no mail at all.

Only half her mind was on the colorful catalogs, the other half on the man in the kitchen who was opening and shutting cabinet doors and whistling something that sounded like a dispute between a mocking bird and a tea kettle.

By the time she'd gone to bed last night they'd barely been speaking. Mac had made a few valiant attempts at conversation, but she'd been afraid to let down her guard, afraid he might try to kiss her again.

Afraid he might not.

Well, this couldn't go on, not as long as they were sharing a house. They were both sensible adults, after all. She needed to keep reminding herself of that fact.

At least, one of them was. "Mac? Did you know you can actually buy wheelchairs by mail?"

He called through the hall from the kitchen. "Never given it much thought. Why, you in the market for one?"

When he appeared in the doorway behind her, she flashed him a grin over her shoulder. "No, but I was just thinking—with mail order and the Internet, there's no real reason why a woman couldn't live here for the rest of her life without ever having to leave the island.''

There, that hadn't been so hard. At least they were conversing comfortably again.

Sending her a curious look, he came on inside the room. "You planning on it?"

She shrugged. "I don't know. Maybe."

"Here? I mean, in this particular house?"

"Why not? It's mine. Marian called it a fixer-upper, but why bother to fix it up if I'm not going to live here?"

"You could rent it. The whole house, I mean, not just the back part."

"Then I'd have to find another place to live. It would probably end up costing me all the rent I received, so what's the advantage?"

Wearing baggy cargo pants that still managed to hug his narrow hips, he lowered himself onto the sofa, leaned forward and rested his arms on his knees. She could feel her face flushing as she wondered if he was thinking about that kiss.

Obviously, he wasn't. "What would you do?" he asked.

"With my time, you mean? Well, first of all I'd have to find a job. As for leisure time, I don't surf, I don't fish, but there're all sorts of opportunities for volunteers. I might even paint my house, maybe a pale shade of yellow with black shutters. Or maybe classic white again, with dark green. I'll have to think about it. And landscaping. I have some definite ideas there.''

He looked at her as if he were trying to picture her as a permanent resident, or maybe a house painter. Actually, she couldn't quite bring it into focus yet either, but the more she thought about it, the more she liked the idea of living here. Roots had to count for something.

''Okay, the painting can wait another year, but maybe I can get started planting a few things. Seeds don't cost much.''

He looked at her and said nothing. ''Well, everyone has to live somewhere,'' she reasoned. ''I'm already here and settled in.''

He toyed with a screwdriver, twirling the business end against the palm of his hand. One curt nod, and then, ''What kind of job?''

''Cleaning cottages,'' she said, hoping he wouldn't laugh.

He didn't have to. The look he sent her spoke volumes, none of it particularly flattering. Lines from an old musical popped into her mind. ''Anything you can do, I can do better.'' She couldn't remember who the singer had been—Ethel Merman? Debbie Reynolds?—but the rebuttal had been, ''No, you can't,'' followed promptly by, ''Yes, I can.''

My sentiments exactly, Val thought, feeling oddly let down when he got up and left without a word.

By the time she'd finished going through her junk mail, the sun was sparkling like diamonds on the whole outside world. Stiff from sitting in one place too long, she rose, stretched and wandered to the door for a better look. The outside air had been cool earlier. Now it felt almost balmy. She considered opening a few windows to let the warm breeze blow through the house, and then thought of all the work of taking down and stapling up the plastic again.

Back to the drawing board. Or in this case, the coffee table. Once she finished with the flyers and catalogs she turned back to the files. The first one she picked up was filled with property-tax-related correspondence, most of it bearing her father's enigmatic notations. Oddly enough, in the middle of his personal medical records she came across several insurance-related letters addressed to Ms. Mitty Stoddard, dated over a period of four years. Why would her father have had access to those? As an employee, she'd been eligible for the standard company benefits package.

There were several more items pertaining to Mitty L. Stoddard, most of them form letters that should have been thrown away. Instead, they'd been squeezed into the middle of other folders. Mitty L. Stoddard. Matilda Lyford? That name had shown up on several documents. Could they possibly be one and the same?

Val was astonished at how much she had taken for granted about people she'd known half her life. Her father might have intended to start a Miss Mitty file like the ones he'd kept for Charlie and Belinda— although why he should, she couldn't imagine. Even

Charlie and Belinda were insured under the company's umbrella.

Whatever his intent had been, she only hoped Miss Mitty had taken her full retirement package with her when she'd left. Back in August of last year that shouldn't have been a problem, as the trouble hadn't even shown up until a few months later.

More confused than ever, Val tossed the file she'd been examining back in the box, flexed her shoulders and yawned. She needed an oxygen break. Briefly she considered seeing if Mac needed a hand with whatever he was doing, then thought better of it. She'd missed Marian this morning, but it was now after one. If nothing else, it was a valid excuse to enjoy a midwinter spring day while it lasted.

She was still wearing the ivory suede slacks she'd put on this morning. They were creased, but she decided against changing. Instead of the thick, Peruvian knit sweater though, she changed into a peasant top that was fresh off the catwalk, but casual enough to have come from a discount store. Amused, she wondered if there was such a thing as a reverse snob.

On her way out, she found Mac up on the ladder, poking gobs of rotted leaves out of the gutter with a stick. "I'm going out. Do you need anything?"

"Dozen eggs," he said, looking down from his shaky Mount Olympus. His feet were braced on either side of the rung. The view from where she stood was spectacular, to put it mildly.

"They'll ruin your heart."

"I'll drink an extra beer to make up for it."

"Fine, Dr. MacBride, you just do that." They'd both read the article in a recent *Virginian Pilot* on drinking and its relationship to heart health.

He grinned down at her. She flipped him a wave and crossed the soggy lawn to her car, thankful that they were back on the old standing. Something more, perhaps, than before, but still within safe limitations. Nothing she couldn't handle.

Marian was in, and so was her daughter Tracy, a five-year-old with her mother's beautiful smile, minus a few teeth.

"I came about that job," Val said after greetings and introductions. "If it's still available, I'll take it, but you'll have to tell me what's expected. Believe it or not, I'm pretty good at following written instructions."

"I believe it. I meant to stop in a time or two to see how you were getting along, but now that we're into February things are starting to heat up, reservation-wise. So…how've you been doing?"

"Great. Much better since you sent me my handyman. He's a genius."

Without looking away from Val, Marian handed Tracy a yellow crayon. "What handyman?"

Seven

Twenty-five minutes later Val wheeled in off the highway, skidded on the wet grass and parked under the live oak tree. The ladder was gone. There was no sign of MacBride.

Damn him, who *was* he? Why had he lied to her? His car was still here. She'd half expected him to have fled.

Drumming on the steering wheel, she rehearsed the questions she intended to ask—no, to demand answers to. It didn't help when she noticed that her last two unbroken fingernails had been nibbled to the quick.

She *hated* this! They had just been getting to know each other. Talking, exploring—feeling their way. As for the kiss, she dismissed it as an impulse. Tried to, anyway.

All right, so maybe talking wasn't all she was interested in, but he'd lied to her, and that she could not forgive. Social lies—small lies intended to spare someone's feelings—those were occasionally necessary, but the intent of MacBride's lie had clearly been to deceive. There was never an excuse for that.

Feeling raw and shaky, she got out, closed the car door quietly behind her and strode toward the house, chin held high, back stiff as a palace guard. This was *her* house, she reminded herself. She could kick him out first, or she could demand an explanation and then kick him out.

Just as she swung the front door wide, Mac came in through the back, holding a length of black hose in one hand. "Notice how easy the door is to open?" The stubble on his lower face did nothing to minimize the effect of his smile.

She glared at him.

His smile faded. He lifted one eyebrow. Nodding to the hose he still held, he said, "Found your culprit." His eyes narrowed as he took in her frozen expression. "Hey, I was just kidding about the beer, you didn't have to make a special trip just for that."

She wasn't carrying any beer. It was a wonder she'd even remembered to retrieve her purse from Marian's desk. "Would you mind telling me who the devil you are and what you're doing in my house?" She tried for cool composure and missed by a country mile.

He took a step back, eyeing her the way he might some exotic reptile he'd found coiled in his bed. "John Leo MacBride? Checking out your leaky washer?" He turned both statements into questions, as if wondering how much of his story she would buy.

She'd already bought far more than she could afford. "Marian at Seaview never heard of you. She didn't send you. How did you know I needed a handyman?"

"You told me."

Her mouth fell open. "*I* told you. And just when did I do that?"

"Six days—maybe a week ago? You took down the calendar, how'm I supposed to keep up with what day it is?"

Nice try, but she wasn't buying it. He had a perfectly good watch that told him everything he needed to know, probably including the Dow Jones futures. Besides, the actual date had nothing to do with the big, fat lie he'd told her. "It was last year's calendar. Try again."

Without even glancing at the hose that appeared to have been mended with tape on the curved end, he hung it over the doorknob. "When I saw your sign and came to the door to inquire about the room for rent."

Her brain did a quick double take. Damn, damn, damn! The sign she'd meant to take down and had never gotten around to. She hated being caught in the wrong, especially when she was certain she was right. Basically right, anyway.

Desperately, she tried to recall everything she'd said that first day, as well as what his responses had been, but too much time had elapsed. It seemed more like weeks, or even months than mere days.

She narrowed a look at the man who had settled so comfortably into her house, carving out a place for himself in her life. At the rate they'd been progressing, she was lucky he hadn't already claimed a place in her bed. She'd like to think she had better sense, but the way she'd been acting lately, all bets were off.

What now? Miss Manners didn't cover this kind of situation. Taking a slow, calming breath, she said, "You're claiming it was a simple misunderstanding?"

He shrugged. "What else? I happened to be in the area, I needed a place to stay, I saw your sign."

It was just barely plausible. "And decided to apply for a job as handyman?" The need for one was certainly obvious enough, even if she hadn't launched on a list of all that needed doing.

"You needed help. I happened to be available."

She gnawed her lip, uncertain where to go from here. No matter what he claimed, he was no simple handyman. A reporter would have asked more questions. He hadn't mentioned Greenwich, much less BFC, which was hardly worth a journalist's time anyway at this point.

He stood patiently while she looked him over from

the tips of his top-quality, but well-worn deck shoes to the crown of his shaggy, sun-bleached hair. A federal agent? Hardly. Every government agent she'd ever met wore dark, nondescript suits and bad ties. Besides, why bother? "All right," she said finally, trying to sound as if she had everything under control.

She had nothing under control. Not long ago she had cleaned out her bank account, signed dozens of documents, left the keys to her father's house with her personal banker and headed south in a second-hand car filled with impractical clothes, sentimental trinkets and stolen files. She'd had the misguided notion that getting away from the scene of so many painful memories would give her the objectivity she needed to get to the bottom of the mystery and restore her father's reputation.

So far, she hadn't found one blasted thing relating to BFC and the supposedly missing money. She couldn't even swear the money was missing, although if not, someone had an awful lot to answer for.

For all she knew, some minor accountant in the throes of a mid-life crisis had dreamed up the whole thing. Or maybe a computer virus was responsible. If viruses could make everything on a computer disappear, hiding millions of dollars should be easy. Either that or Robin Hood had cleaned out the coffers and donated everything to the United Fund.

Oh, Lord, she was no longer certain of anything

except that Mac was waiting for some sort of a response and her brain had turned to vichyssoise.

"Valerie?"

"All right," she said firmly in an effort to regain the upper hand. "Honesty compels me to accept part of the blame. I should never have hired you without asking for references, I just wasn't thinking clearly that day."

"Next time, ask for references and a deposit."

"You're *lecturing* me?"

"Only offering a suggestion. Now…do you want a brief biography? Character references? I think we're square on the deposit for now. A week's work in exchange for a week's rent."

He knew exactly how long it had been, which was more than she did.

She moved into the kitchen and he followed her there. She pulled out a chair and sat. He remained standing. She said, "The other day when you were sharpening the weed whacker—I asked you about your sweatshirt, remember?"

He nodded warily.

"Instead of answering a simple question we ended up talking about history, of all things." She should have known then that he was something more than he appeared to be, although what he appeared to be was impressive enough.

"Here? Right here? But what about the Pilgrims?" she remembered asking.

"Not that batch, the ones that came before."

She'd pointed to the ground beside her sheepskin-lined boots. "You're telling me they landed right where we're standing right now?" History happened to be one of her weaker subjects, but at that point, if he'd wanted to discuss Martian invaders, she probably would have listened avidly as long as she could watch the muscles in his bared forearms tense and relax with each stroke of the sharpening tool.

"Close. Advance guard stopped off a few miles up the beach to ask directions of a few friendly natives. Ended up settling a few miles northwest of here on Roanoke Island. Hand me that hatchet, will you? Might as well sharpen that, too, while I'm at it."

"But I thought—what about the Pilgrims? The *Mayflower*?"

He'd grinned that slow-burner grin of his and said, "Sorry to disillusion you, but we Yankees wrote the textbooks, so we got to slant history our way. Doesn't necessarily mean it happened that way."

"You're saying truth is relative?"

"Now you're getting into philosophy," he'd dismissed with another contagious grin. "That was never my strong suit. I guess what I'm saying is that truth is what actually takes place. How you interpret it depends on where you happen to be standing."

Was it her imagination, or had he studied her face intently at that point, almost as if he were waiting for a particular reaction? A few moments later he'd shrugged and gone on sharpening the rusty old tools he'd found under layers of junk in her cluttered shed, leaving her wondering more than ever what he was doing working as a handyman.

All right, she thought now, so the truth was relative. She'd settle for a single particle of truth about John Leo MacBride, just one. Up until today he'd been simply a fascinating, increasingly tempting, surprisingly complex man who seemed informed on a number of topics. One who could kiss like a dream and then back away, leaving a woman hungry for more, she reminded herself. What was it they always labeled boxes of dynamite with—XXX? Or was that sugar?

He was triple-X doubled, on both counts.

Leaning against a counter, he grinned. "Know what this reminds me of? Remember that old movie, *Showdown at the O.K. Coral?*"

She purposefully kept her expression blank. She'd happened to mention enjoying old movies one night recently when he'd brought up the absence of a TV.

"You know the one," he prompted, as cheerfully as if his employment weren't hanging by a thread. "Couple of gunfighters facing off in the middle of the main drag while the townspeople huddle behind saloon doors?"

"It was *Gunfight,* not *Showdown,*" she said tightly.

He didn't crack a smile, but his eyes sparkled like wet amber.

Outside the kitchen window a flock of cedar waxwings swarmed into a yaupon tree, then took flight again. Momentarily distracted, she followed their movement before looking back. He was still leaning against the counter, arms crossed over his chest, one foot propped over the other, as if this were just another casual conversation.

"Yes, well," she said. "To get back to what we were discussing, I might have jumped to the wrong conclusion, but you didn't do one thing to set me straight." Had she even given him time to explain who he was before launching into a litany of what needed doing first? Probably not—she'd been tired, desperate and totally out of her depth at the time.

"I can leave now if you'd like," he said quietly.

She was half tempted to take him up on it. Probably be better off if she did. "Give me a minute, let me think about it."

For all the good thinking did. There was simply no rational way to explain the effect he had on her. This one man among all the other men she'd ever met, including the one she had almost married.

In desperation, she latched onto the least important part of their relationship. One more day and he would have started paying rent. Aside from everything else, she needed that money. Even if she threw him out and advertised for another tenant, who was to say the next one would be any better?

Well…he could hardly be better. The trouble was, the next tenant might be a whole lot worse.

"I can be out of here in five minutes," he repeated when the silence stretched to the breaking point. "Ten, if you want me to make a list of what still needs doing."

"I thought we were pretty well caught up."

"There's still those boards under your washer that

need replacing, and I haven't done the flashing yet, remember? Dare Building had to order stuff.''

''I guess I owe you for materials,'' she said reluctantly. And for last night's supper and for all the hours of fascinating conversations that had enabled her to justify putting off what she'd come here to do.

''No problem. I opened an account at Dare and charged everything to you. They knew your great-grandmother.''

She gnawed on a ragged nail, then caught herself and slid her hand guiltily under her thigh. She'd like to blame the rapidly changing weather for her inability to focus, but she knew better.

''You need a new hose for your washer, by the way, but the patch should hold until you can order one. I cleaned out the filter while I was at it. Thing was pretty well clogged with sand. You might want to do that from time to time. I can show you where it's located.''

Dammit, why did you kiss me? Did I look like I needed kissing? Like I was desperate for affection? For sex?

She flung out her hands in surrender. ''Oh, for heaven's sake, stay! It was my mistake after all, not yours.''

He waited so long she was afraid he was going to insist on leaving. She couldn't blame him after she'd insulted his integrity…or whatever it was she'd insulted. Certainly not his masculinity, that had never been in question.

''Speaking of mistakes,'' he said in that deep,

calm voice that shivered over her skin like the stroke of an ostrich plume, "Next time you rent your rooms, be sure to ask for a deposit up front in case your tenant trashes the place or walks out owing you money."

"I knew that," she snapped. "You already reminded me."

"Then I'll pay you a deposit now. We never got around to discussing how much rent you're asking."

"We never got around to discussing your hourly rate."

He nodded, but said nothing. Val lacked the patience to deal with another stalemate. "A thousand?"

He whistled quietly. "A month? A year? With or without kitchen privileges?"

She visualized the cramped, poorly furnished room and the barely adequate bath. "Let me ask my friend at the agency. This place was one of her listings until I moved in. She'll know the local rates."

Marian had been surprised and more than a little uneasy when Val had told her about her handy tenant and the agreement they'd struck. By the time they'd finished discussing the matter, Val had been furious, frightened and embarrassed. Not to mention disappointed. "I don't think he's a—a beach bum, if that's what you mean," she'd said.

"What about a dangerous escaped convict?" Marian had been joking, but Val had to admit that Mac-Bride was dangerous, if not the kind of threat Marian had had in mind.

"If a personal check will do, I'll give you a deposit now," Mac repeated.

"You have a bank account?" That indicated a certain degree of stability, didn't it? Even if the check bounced.

"Not here—in Mystic. Will that do?"

Mystic. He'd told her only that he was from New England. She wanted to know everything there was to know about him, but that could wait.

He was still standing; she was still seated. She wasn't sure which, in this case, was the dominant position, but she evened the odds by standing. "I'll let you know what the rent is as soon as I find out. If you'd like to pay a deposit, then I think we should do it properly. References, lease—that sort of thing. I'll have to get a copy of a lease form from Marian."

"Short term lease," he stipulated.

"Of course," she said quickly.

With a few added clauses: from now on, we'll stick strictly to business. No more cozy chats by the fireside, no more beach walks in the rain. Definitely no more kisses and accidental-on-purpose touches.

He nodded. "It might take a few days to get written references from my last residence."

"Fine. In the meantime, you know what needs doing." She turned to go, then added, "Oh, and by the way, I'll be working, starting tomorrow."

"Working. Outside the house, you mean?"

"I told you I was considering it. I'll be cleaning cottages on weekends between check-out and check-in. Mostly Saturday and Sunday mornings. So,'' she said airily—once again captain of her own ship, CEO of her own affairs. ''If you don't mind hooking up that hose thingy, I'd like to do a load of laundry.''

Eight

Later that night Mac, arms crossed under his head, stretched out on the hard bed. It no longer sagged, thanks to a sheet of plywood between mattress and springs. An unseasonably warm wind whistled through the window, rippling the light spread over his boxer-clad body. All that ladder work, not to mention crawling around under the house, hadn't helped his knee.

But a stiff knee was the least of his problems. What the devil was he going to do now? Admit that he was here on a mission that had nothing to do with leaky washing machines and clogged drains? That she had something he wanted, and one way or another, he was determined to get it?

Unfortunately, what he wanted most of all was the

woman herself, and that wasn't going to happen. His conscience alone would prevent it as long as he kept reminding himself that any evidence he might find to clear his stepbrother was bound to condemn her late father.

Hell, she had to know Bonnard was guilty, even if she didn't want to believe it. Loyalty was an admirable trait, but occasionally, it was misplaced.

Probably misplaced, he amended.

Restlessly, he got out of bed and stood at the window, staring out at the million or so stars that twinkled through a ghostly stand of dead pines, lingering victims of Hurricane Emily, or so he'd been told.

Recalling his very first dive off Cozumel back in the early seventies, he had to admit that even the evidence of his own eyes could sometimes be misleading. He'd seen what had appeared to be a five-gallon Coke bottle under some fifty feet of crystal-clear water and gone down after it. Green kid, first dive, rented equipment that would probably never have passed inspection. A few minutes later he'd surfaced holding an ordinary six-ounce Coke bottle. Layers of glass-like water had acted as a lens, magnifying its size. That's when he'd first learned that what you see is not necessarily what you get.

What if Frank Bonnard hadn't been guilty, after all? The man had barely had time to profess his innocence, much less to prove it, before he'd died. And without a paying client, his lawyer wasn't shaking any trees. So far as Mac knew, Val Bonnard was the only one who believed in her father's innocence.

Rumor was that he'd died on her thirtieth birthday. If so, that made it doubly rough. Losing a father was never easy, but losing him like that had to have been a staggering blow. According to Will, in only a matter of weeks she'd lost not only her father, but her home, her wealth and her family's reputation.

Mac had to admit that under the circumstances, she was doing a pretty fine job of rolling with the punches.

It wasn't the sun streaming into the room that awakened her, it was the sound of thumping and hammering. Val glanced at her watch and groaned. She'd meant to get an early start today, so as to go through a few more files before she had to leave for her first day as a cottage-cleaner.

Still groggy from a restless night, she felt her way downstairs to find that Mac had shoved the washer aside and was already at work ripping out the floor. Before she went to bed last night she'd used the machine. Thanks to the mended hose, it hadn't overflowed again.

Even so she was half tempted to send him packing for the simple reason that every time she looked at him her hormones overruled the few grains of common sense she'd managed to hang on to.

"Sorry. Did I wake you?" Down on one knee, he was leaning over a hole in the floor, baring a band of tanned flesh between sweatshirt and jeans.

She stared, blinked, mumbled "G'morning" and backed out of the small utility room, which was actually little more than a shallow closet off the hallway.

There was a frying pan on the stove, used dishes stacked neatly in the sink, and two pieces of cold bacon on a paper towel. She nibbled on one while she made toast. Not bothering to make tea, she poured herself a cup of coffee from the carafe on the warming plate, added half-and-half and two spoonfuls of sugar, and took the lot into the living room.

Reluctantly, she lifted three files from the right side of the box—ones she hadn't yet searched, as she'd been working from left to right. It had seemed logical for reasons that now escaped her.

Why not start in the middle and work in both directions? With such a total lack of organizational skills, how on earth had her father managed to pull together a company that, while it hadn't been among the Fortune 500, might eventually have rated a listing among someone's top ten thousand?

It wasn't enough that he misfiled everything from old brokerage statements to veterinarian's bills for a cat that had died of old age the year she had moved from Chicago to New York—he had scribbled across the face of half the papers in the file. Sums, initials, odd things like, Check yesterday, and Call Tv. Agnt.

Television agent? Travel agent? But why? Her father hadn't taken a vacation in years, which was probably one of the reasons he'd died. The first bit of stress and he'd keeled over.

"Dammit, dammit," she muttered. She would not cry, she would not!

"You say something?" Mac called from the back hallway.

"No, go back to what you were doing."

Her untouched coffee had grown cold by the time she'd gone through each file twice. In the last few she'd examined there'd been several references to BFC, none of which she'd understood and all of which bore those enigmatic notations.

Dad, I know you didn't deliberately do anything wrong, but how do you expect me to prove it with the mess I've got here? Maybe if you'd done a better job of keeping records....

Or maybe if she'd turned the lot over to the experts....

"Or to a fortuneteller," she said, shaking her head. "Oh, darn." One glance at her watch and she realized she would have to choose between an early lunch and an early start.

As this was her first day on the job she chose the early start. Dashing upstairs, she dressed quickly in a Save the Whales sweatshirt, a pair of Diesel jeans that now bagged a full inch around her waistline, and her most comfortable tennis shoes. Chances were fairly good she wouldn't be playing tennis anytime soon.

Mac was in the kitchen when she went downstairs. He'd evidently finished the floor, as he'd shoved the washer back in place. "Lunch is ready," he called out just as she reached for her anorak.

"Don't have time."

"Take time. You'll work better with a little energy food."

Her stomach reminded her that a slice of toast, a strip of cold bacon and half a cup of coffee were only memories, and not altogether pleasant ones, at that. "Oh, all right. I guess I can spare ten minutes."

Lunch was canned ravioli and bagged salad. One whiff of tomato sauce and she was suddenly ravenous. She slid into a chair while Mac set out the plates and handed her a canister of grated cheese.

"You need any help?" he inquired.

"Why should I need help? It's only housecleaning. You think I don't know how?" Belligerence didn't come naturally to her, she had to work at it.

"Just offering," he said calmly.

She doused her salad with olive oil and dribbled on balsamic vinegar. "Thanks for lunch," she said grudgingly.

"I'll check the attic again while you're gone. Any leaks should show up after yesterday's rain."

Oh, great. What next, a new roof? She sighed and stared at the pattern of tomato sauce on her plate, then scratched through it with her fork. "I wonder if ravioli sauce is as accurate as tea leaves."

Looking thoughtful, he said, "What counts, I suspect, is the eye of the beholder, not the beheld."

Why was it so impossible to hold a grudge against the man, even when a grudge was justified? Her immune system must be seriously compromised. "My dad used to quote this guy who was famous back in

his college days for saying the medium was the message.''

Mac nodded gravely. ''At that age, ambiguous
phrases often pass for wisdom.''

''I think I prefer something more concrete, such
as, 'Unless otherwise indicated, start at the top, work
toward the bottom, lock the door on your way out.'

''Your orders of the day?''

She nodded, wondering for the first time what that
''unless otherwise indicated'' involved. ''Speaking
of orders of the day, could you possibly take that air
conditioner out of my bedroom window? On days
like this, I'd love to be able to open it and get some
fresh air inside.''

''Will do. Want me to take down the plastic on
the other window?''

She drummed her fingers on the table, then shook
her head. ''Decisions, decisions. Would you mind
making that one for me? I can't worry about too
many things at once, and right now I'm thinking
about what Marian said about things people leave
behind in cottages.''

He chuckled and said, ''Pass the salt.''

They were both making an effort to patch up their
relationship, but it wasn't easy. Not when her gaze
kept straying to his mouth, with its full lower lip and
its carved upper. She couldn't forget how those lips
had felt moving over hers—over her throat, her eyes.
Couldn't help wondering what would have happened
if they hadn't been bundled up in layers of clothing,
with a cold rain blowing in on them.

She raked back her chair abruptly. "I need to leave."

"You're really serious about this?"

She paused in the act of rinsing her plate. "Did you think I wasn't?"

"How long is this job of yours supposed to last?"

"As long as I want it to last. Although if Marian's regular cleaner comes back from maternity leave, I'll have to look for something else." She quickly ran hot water in the sink and squirted lemon-scented liquid detergent. He handed her his plate and cutlery, but held back his cup.

"I might even apply at another rental agency if I like the work," she said, making short work of the wash-up.

"What's not to like about scrubbing and vacuuming?" He pursed his lips, and she really wished he wouldn't. "Good luck, then," he said. "I'll finish a few odd jobs around here and then catch up on my reading. Handyman's day off. I brought along a few books I haven't even unpacked yet."

Setting the rinsed dishes in the drainer, she thought about what it would be like to curl up before an open fire—or even an ugly oil heater—and spend a rainy afternoon together. Reading, talking, listening to music—maybe even napping.

Except that it wasn't raining and she had too much to do, not to mention having better sense than to put herself in jeopardy deliberately.

After a quick dash upstairs to grab her purse and the instructions Marian had given her, she was ready to leave. Time was critical during the season, but this time of year most of the cottages weren't even booked, according to the agent, who'd said, "I'd better warn you, a couple of the places haven't been cleaned since the last renters checked out two weeks ago. You might want to check the refrigerator first thing. Throw out everything, whether or not it's got moss on it."

Calculating quickly as she pulled out onto Back Road, Val figured that if she got through today's list she would have earned just over a hundred dollars. Not long ago, before the collapse of BFC, the death of her father and the collapse of all she'd held dear, that would have been pocket change. Now it meant that after this weekend she might be able to pay for her roofing material. Next weekend's work should probably go toward property taxes. After that she could start saving toward having her septic tank pumped.

If she'd come down here hoping to gain fresh perspective, she'd succeeded beyond her wildest dreams. Now all she had to do was put that perspective to use on those messy, mysterious files, instead of dreaming about yellow clapboards and Cape jasmine bushes, hand-detailed furniture and hand-hooked rugs.

Mac considered starting on the files again after Val drove off. So far he'd made a cursory search through nearly a dozen, reaching the conclusion that Bonnard had been in desperate need of clerical help. Maybe if they were to tackle the job together, bounce ideas off one another, they might make more headway. She knew her father's handwriting and would probably recognize most, if not all of the references.

At least he wouldn't feel quite so guilty. She'd caught him fair on the handyman thing, but she still didn't know the worst. He had put his life on hold until he'd cleared Will. Why hadn't she asked him why he was here? He might even have told her.

Dammit, he wasn't cut out to be a double agent, not even in a worthy cause. For a marine archeologist, he was a pretty good plumber, and not a bad carpenter. When and if he ever had to quit diving, instead of trying for a teaching position he just might open his own handyman business.

Meanwhile, he might check out that maritime museum down in Hatteras village. He'd been intending to all week, but he had an idea that once inside, he might not surface anytime soon. Right now, though, he had a more pressing agenda.

The question was, did he still consider her a suspect? *Remember that five-gallon Coke bottle,* he reminded himself.

The moment he opened her bedroom door, every male hormone in his body went on standby alert. Her scent was a subtle echo, reminding him of a patch of white flowers he'd noticed once when he'd gone down to the University of Miami for a conference. Struck by their fragrance, he'd asked what they were.

Ginger lilies. She smelled of ginger lilies and something else, something intensely personal.

Glancing around, he saw the figurine he'd noticed on the mantel downstairs a few days ago—a china ballerina with one foot propped on a stool, holding the laces of a red shoe in both hands. He remembered thinking at the time that there was something disarming about the tiny painted face.

Great. The last thing he needed at this point was to be disarmed.

He unplugged the air-conditioner unit, lifted it out and eased it onto a chair. She'd told him to store the unit in one of the unused rooms for now, so he crossed the hall and shoved open the door of the room at the head of the stairs. The room had two double-hung windows, both with what was probably the original glass. He lingered a moment in the musty room, looking out through the wavery glass to a marsh, a narrow creek and a steep, wooded ridge. The archeologist in him wondered what was underneath the dunes and ridges. While his ever-curious romantic side imagined a grounded shipwreck collecting sand over the centuries, the realist in him admitted it was far more likely to be a fallen tree, or even a clump of grass. It didn't take a geologist to know that barrier islands were constantly moving.

Closing the door behind him, he returned to her bedroom to close the window, making a mental note to look for a screen. A flash of color caught his attention when he turned to leave. Her closet door hung open. Another project for him to tackle, although, short of leveling the whole house, there wasn't much he could do. Maybe reset the hinges.

His gaze strayed to the colorful array of clothing crammed inside the narrow space. He was no fashion expert, but he figured most of the stuff, while it might be suitable for the country club set she had moved in, wasn't going to do her much good down here. Maybe the blue jeans. The pair she'd been wearing when she'd left could have cost anywhere from ten bucks to a couple of hundred, he was no expert when it came to ladies' clothing. A few months ago they'd probably fit her like a coat of primer, but not anymore. She'd lost weight. Too much worry. Too much physical labor on top of too little sleep.

At least he was seeing that she ate three squares a day now. Before he'd showed up she'd evidently been subsisting on peanut butter and tea.

Her bedroom was directly over his. Instead of claiming the front room with its eastern exposure, she'd chosen one where the sun wouldn't wake her until mid-morning. He could hear her up here at night, rolling and tossing. More than once he'd been tempted to offer his own insomnia cure. Fortunately, his survival instincts had kicked in before he could make a major mistake.

Still, he lingered in the room that smelled of her subtle perfume, staring at the pillow that bore a faint impression of her head. She hadn't made her bed. Probably used to having someone do it for her.

Restlessly, he shifted his stance. Now what? Go through the damned files, or go out and whack some more weeds?

Downstairs, he opened a beer and settled down in

the recliner, determined to discover why she'd
brought these particular folders with her. He figured
he had a minimum of two hours before she got back.
After some forty-five minutes of scanning documents, most of which should long since have been
consigned to the shredder, he stood and stretched,
wondering how a man with the organizational skills
of a three-toed sloth could have managed to rip off
his own company without leaving a whisper of evidence. BFC's computers had immediately been impounded. Bonnard's personal secretary had been
questioned repeatedly, to no avail. According to Will,
the executive offices were still off-limits to all but
authorized police personnel.

And here he was, more than five hundred miles
away, searching through obsolete dental records and
unpaid traffic tickets. One entire folder had been de-
voted to statements from a department store where,
according to Will, Macy regularly maxed out her accounts. Somehow, he couldn't see Val Bonnard letting overdue accounts pile up. Not the way she'd
tackled the stalagmites inside that oven.

On the other hand, he couldn't see Frank Bonnard
running up bills at a place that catered mostly to
women—unless he'd been keeping a mistress on the
side, and there'd been no evidence of that. No evidence of any women in his life other than the daughter and a few close friends, most of whom weren't
exactly arm-candy material.

Damn it, he liked nothing better than a challenge,
but so far, this one had him buffaloed.

He closed the last folder and laid it aside. When it came to thinking like an accountant he was at a disadvantage. His brain simply wasn't wired that way. It didn't help when his thoughts kept straying off the reservation.

He kicked the recliner back another notch and tried not to think about the way her bed had looked, with its rumpled sheets and the thick duvet. Tried not to think about the way it smelled—the lingering scent of white flowers.

Finishing off his beer, he set the bottle on the floor, closed his eyes and made an effort to view the overall situation through the lens of a maritime archeologist faced with the task of locating a well-documented wreck. With Will's help, he'd done the preliminaries before he'd ever left Greenwich, both of them reaching the same obvious conclusion. Trouble was, their conclusion no longer held water. Their damned conclusion had begun to crumble the minute he'd seen her—seen the way she was living.

At first he'd rationalized that she was smarter than he'd given her credit for being, but even that hadn't held up. Too many times he'd seen her face after she'd been holed up in here with the damned files— a mixture of sadness, frustration...even irritation. He'd been tempted more than once to tell her he felt the same way himself. Not the sadness, but the rest of it.

But if he told her that, he'd have to admit he'd been lying to her from the first, by omission if not commission. Whatever her opinion of him was now, it would sink even lower. And dammit, it mattered to him. More than it should. Torn loyalties were the pits.

So ease off on the testosterone and jump-start your brain, jerk!

Even a disinterested spectator would be forced to concede that Bonnard hadn't dug a hole under his cabbage patch and buried his plunder. Nor had he shoveled a ton of gold bullion down a coal chute to his basement. The question remained—how the devil had he pulled it off? If he'd been skimming profits over a matter of years, why hadn't anyone noticed? These were professional number-crunchers whose sole purpose was to invest money for maximum profits, see that it was properly allocated and that none of it, other than legitimately earned commissions, went astray. If any money had followed her here, she'd been damned clever at hiding it.

Granted, there was that closet full of fancy clothes upstairs. And her watch—the only jewelry she wore—was a good one. Even so, it had probably cost less than his old stainless-steel Submariner. From what he knew of Val Bonnard—and he was getting to know her far better than he'd ever intended—material things weren't that important to her. Not if she was thinking about keeping this old relic of a house and making the kind of improvements she'd been talking about recently. Cape jasmine bushes on each side of the porch and a fresh paint job?

The most telling of all, though, was the fact that she was cleaning cottages. Hell, he didn't even want her cleaning this one. Her hands were a mess—she had blisters on top of blisters. Some of that stuff she was breathing, she probably needed a mask for.

He had started out wondering how far a guilty woman would go to cover her tracks. At this point he was all but convinced that not only wasn't she a part of the scam, she honestly believed in her father's innocence.

Which meant that, in her own way, she was as much a victim as Will.

Nine

Mac stood and glared at the white satin ballet slippers half hidden under the sofa. What in God's name, he wondered, had made him offer to play detective? He didn't have the right mindset, much less the right skills. Not in this century. Not when real, live people were involved, people he cared about. People who wore ballet slippers and muttered ladylike curses at a dirty oven.

Flipping the last file into the box, he thought about getting himself another beer, but he'd already had two. He was having enough trouble keeping his mind on track without blurring the edges with alcohol. He'd never been much of a drinker, mindful of the familiar warning that drinking and diving don't mix.

"Okay, MacBride, put it in perspective. Small

company, fewer than half a dozen employees in a position to cook the books.''

The most likely candidate, CFO Sam Hutchinson, had been turned inside out and given a clean bill of health. Next most likely was in no condition to testify, at least not in any earthly court. If Bonnard had hoped to escape paying taxes, he'd succeeded...the hard way.

For the first time Mac wondered if Will could have pulled it off. Opportunity wouldn't have been a problem. As for motivation, one had to look no further than Macy, who had left him as soon as she'd realized that any accountant whose name was even whispered in context with a financial scandal might as well look for a job bagging groceries.

Will had started out as an accountant shortly before he and Macy were married, then had worked his way through law school with Macy cracking the whip. A small-town beauty queen, she'd been working as a paralegal when they'd met. Macy had always been more ambitious than her husband.

Will had practiced law for less than two years and had hated every hour of it. So when the opening at BFC had come along with its promise of advancement, she'd relented and let him off the hook, law-wise.

So yeah—Will had to be seen as a candidate. Trouble was, he couldn't lie. Even as a kid he'd turned red-faced and glassy-eyed whenever he'd tried to lie his way out of some minor indiscretion.

Back to Bonnard, then. Which meant back to Val.

And dammit, he didn't want her involved. He wanted her free to build a new life for herself with no messy ties to the past. With room somewhere in that new life for a freelance diver, a marine archeologist who was motivated more by intellectual curiosity than ambition.

Okay, he'd passed that hurdle—he'd admitted it, to himself, at least.

Closing his eyes, Mac allowed himself to consider various possibilities and probabilities, keeping in mind that six-ounce pop bottle that had been magnified out of all proportion. He was almost asleep when Val burst through the front door.

"Did you know it's raining again? I can't believe this crazy weather! Mac?" She was staring at the folders that had slipped off his lap, scattering papers across the floor. "What's that? What are you doing?"

Oh, hell. Crunch time. He could lie and tell her the tooth fairy left them on his lap while he was napping or he could give his conscience a break and tell her the truth.

"Mac?" She was standing just inside the door looking pale, grimy and exhausted, her dark braid half unraveled, damp tendrils clinging to her face.

"You're wet." Caught off guard, he took the easy way out and stated the obvious.

"My car wouldn't start. I had to flag down a jumper. Mac, what are you doing with my private papers?"

"Would you believe I was trying to figure out how to build you a file drawer?"

"No."

"I didn't think so. Look, there's no easy way to say this—"

"Try the truth for a change." She kicked off her sand-caked shoes and came inside the room. Sinking down onto the sofa, she folded the ends of the duvet over her lap. The temperature was probably up into the high fifties outside, but she was wet and shivering.

"Truth, whole truth, nothing but the truth. Okay, my name really is MacBride. But my stepbrother's name is Will Jordan." He waited for the implication to sink in. She'd been pale before. Now her face lost the last vestige of color. "Would you have given me a chance if I'd told you up front who I was?"

Spanish-moss-gray eyes darkened visibly. "I'd have—" She took a deep, shuddering breath and started over. "I might have. No, I probably wouldn't. But why?" she begged plaintively. "I mean, why are you even here? You're obviously not a handyman looking for work."

He felt like the lowest form of life. There was no excuse for what he'd done. Or rather, there was, but somewhere along the way he'd become entangled in his own motivation. Now, like the tentacles of a Portuguese man o' war, those motives were threatening to do him serious harm.

"Why were you going through my personal papers?'' she repeated when long moments ticked by in silence. Her voice was too quiet, too controlled.

''Because Will's not an embezzler.'' He waited for her reaction. Wouldn't blame her if she kicked his ass out the door and threw his gear out after him. From the way she was looking at him, she was seriously considering it.

''You don't know that,'' she said finally. ''Nobody wants to believe their relative could do anything dishonest.''

''Yeah, I do know it. Val, whoever ripped off your father's company, it wasn't Will. For one thing, money doesn't mean that much to him, even though maximizing profits is probably part of his job description. Was, I should say. Career-wise, he's pretty well washed up.''

Her searching eyes never left his face. She took another deep breath and said, ''My father was not a thief. I don't care what they're saying about him, I knew him better than anyone else, and one thing he was incapable of doing was lying. He never stole so much as a—a book of matches. Money was never what motivated him—not for himself, at least.''

Mac wondered if she realized what that admission implied. ''I'll have to take your word for it. I never met the man.''

Other than the fact that he'd lived in a pretty ritzy part of town and drove a classic Bentley, Frank Bonnard hadn't struck him as a conspicuous consumer. Not like some men who earned considerably less, Will included. But that was Macy's doing.

She sneezed, sniffed, and stood. "I need a tissue."

"You need a hot bath and something to eat."

"Hot tea."

He grimaced. "Go get clean—put on something warm and dry. I'll have the kettle boiling when you come down again. We'll talk."

"We're going to talk, all right," she said grimly. "Don't think you're getting off this easy."

Easy? There was little she could do to him that his own conscience hadn't already done.

He watched her leave, her damp socks leaving small cloudy footprints on the dark varnished floor. *Oh, lady, why couldn't you have been what I started out believing you were? Shallow, spoiled, greedy— crooked as a corkscrew?*

Before heading upstairs, Val tossed her muddy sneakers on top of the washing machine. If she'd been alone in the house she'd have peeled down to the skin, cold or not, and left everything there. What a rotten stinker this whole day had turned out to be. Her first day on the job...and now this.

It wasn't enough that she'd had to deal with some unidentifiable substance left in the sink to grow mold and attract bugs. It wasn't enough that some creep had spilled a sticky drink on an upholstered chair that had run down onto the floor, and in cleaning it up, she'd crawled through the gunk and backed halfway across the floor, leaving a trail of sticky knee prints.

And after all that, to come home to this. Damn him! Damn him all to hell and back, how *dare* he do this to her! Not once, but twice. What was that old saying—fool me once, shame on you; fool me twice, shame on me.

She should have known. Whenever a man went out of his way to be charming, it usually meant he wanted something. Not that Mac had gone out of his way to be charming—he hadn't had to. She'd been easy prey, she admitted reluctantly as she collected a change of clothes from her bedroom.

How had he charmed her? Let me count the ways, she thought bitterly. By drinking the hot tea he despised with barely a grimace. By fascinating her with tales of historic shipping lanes and early colonial settlements, making her forget that she was so tired every bone in her body ached. By making her listen to the whispery flight of the cormorants. By making her laugh when laughing was the last thing she felt like doing. Wasn't it enough that he'd crawled up in her attic and under her house, doing all the grungy things she'd never even had to think of before in exchange for a rust-stained shower and a sagging bed?

Damn him for being so tempting—and herself for being so gullible.

She ran the tub full of tea-colored water that was steamy hot, thanks to her handy-dandy, double-dealing tenant. She dumped in a handful of bath salts, and then another one, just because she needed to make a gesture. Probably slip and break her neck getting out.

Serve her right.

She sank into the welcome warmth, lifted her face and closed her eyes as clouds of fragrant steam rose around her. *Stress, be gone,* she willed silently. Felicity would have had her chanting mantras. Felicity was into the latest version of New Age. Sandy, already a borderline alcoholic, would have poured her a stiff drink and reminded her that life was too short—she might as well enjoy what she could, while she could.

Lacking such help from her friends, Val slipped down until her hair floated around her shoulders. She had barely enough energy to manage a bath. A separate shampoo, complete with conditioner, roller drying and all the rest of her old routine, was out of the question.

Downstairs, Mac waited until he heard the water gurgling down the drain to fill the kettle and switch on a burner. Then he rummaged in the refrigerator for sandwich makings. She needed energy food. Carbohydrates were supposed to be calming, weren't they? Hadn't he read that somewhere?

Setting out store-bought chocolate cookies, bread, pastrami, cheese and a variety of condiments, he noticed the note he'd left for her, anchored with the salt shaker. He'd taken the call shortly after she'd driven off, promising the caller to give her the message as soon as she returned.

Not surprisingly, it had slipped his mind. On first hearing the name *Mitty Stoddard* he'd had a sinking feeling that things were about to go from bad to worse. Although from Val's point of view—his, too, come to think of it—they probably couldn't get much worse.

He smelled her before he heard her. Not that her scent was blatant, it was more a case of his being sensitized. *Susceptible* might be a better term.

"Come sit, drink some tea, eat a bite and then you might want to return the call that came just after you left."

She was wearing a fuzzy pink outfit that didn't deserve to be called sweats, but probably was. He waited for her to read the message.

She scanned it, caught her breath and lifted a pair of gleaming moss-colored eyes. "You talked to her? Was she—did she sound all right? I've been so worried."

"Briefly," he said. "She wanted to know where you were, and I told her you'd gone out for a couple of hours. Then she wanted to know who I was, and I told her—"

"You told her what? That you were Will Jordan's brother?"

"Stepbrother." He shook his head. "I told her I was doing some house repairs for you."

"That's all?"

He jerked a chair from under the table and straddled it. "Look, whether you believe me or not, I'm not in the habit of deceiving people. But neither am I in the habit of broadcasting my private business to strangers."

"Miss Mitty's not a stranger. You knew I'd been trying to get in touch with her."

"I knew you'd called several times. I suspected you were worried, and yes, I knew she used to work for your father." According to Will, Mitty Stoddard was an over-the-hill busybody who'd guarded Frank Bonnard like a junkyard dog with a juicy bone. Also according to Will, Bonnard's secretary might even have had a hand in the lady's early retirement, if being figuratively shoved out the door at the age of seventy-two could be called early retirement. Will didn't know quite how, and Mac considered the whole topic irrelevant.

Leaving a half-made sandwich and taking her tea with her, Val hurried into the next room. Mac could hear her punching in numbers and muttering under her breath. Then he heard, "Miss Mitty? Oh, thank goodness! I can't tell you how worried I've been."

He stepped out onto the back porch to give her some privacy. Eavesdropping was a cut below what even he would stoop to. He'd already stooped pretty low, but he'd like to think he was too honorable to dance this particular version of the limbo.

The rain had slowed to a drizzle so he went and padlocked the shed he'd left open earlier. No reason why—there was nothing of value inside—it was just something to do. Then he stopped by her car, ran a visual check on her tire pressure and did the same to his Land Cruiser. There was just enough light left to see by. When he figured he'd given her enough time, he went back inside, noisily shutting the back door. He was damp, disgruntled and curious.

She met him in the kitchen. "Is your friend all right?" he asked.

Her cheeks were flushed, the blotches of color standing out against her pallor. "She is now. Well, not really—at her age…" She shook her head, dislodging the towel she'd been wearing like a turban.

Unwilling to press her, he switched on the burner to heat more water for tea. The sandwich makings were still on the table. He waited, sensing that she needed to talk, and, as his were the only available ears, chances were he wouldn't even need to prime the pump.

"She broke her hip. That's why I couldn't get in touch with her for so long, she was in this rehabilitation center after she got out of the hospital, and didn't want to worry me with everything else that was going on. Her niece could've called me. I forgot to ask why she hadn't, but then, being practically without a phone for almost a week…"

"Make your sandwich, you need food. Or I'll make it for you."

While she was smearing bread with mustard and horseradish, he pulled up a chair across the table. "Did she know about your father? Will said she retired before the—that is, a while back."

Between big hungry bites, Val told him about Miss Mitty, her father's all-around assistant and adviser, who had been almost as much a part of her life as had Belinda, the housekeeper who'd had a big hand in getting her through puberty and adolescence.

"You know, I never realized it before," she said thoughtfully, "but I don't think they particularly liked each other—Belinda and Miss Mitty. They both loved us, though—my father and me—so they never let it show."

He nodded. When the kettle began to simmer, he got up, retrieved a fresh tea bag and filled her cup.

"I was afraid Miss Mitty hadn't heard about Dad, and I'd have to be the one to tell her, but she reads all the news online. She's better with a computer than I ever was, isn't that amazing? I mean, everyone knows how babies are practically born hooked up to the Internet, but women Miss Mitty's age…'' She diluted her tea with milk and spooned in sugar. "It's just a shame her bones aren't as flexible as her mind."

They talked some more, but it was obvious that she was exhausted. "Leave everything," he told her. "I'll wash up and put away. Either go to bed or go relax in the living room."

"Oh, no," she said, and stifled a yawn. "You're not getting rid of me that easily. We still need to talk about why you were snooping through my files."

"Ouch. Could we retract the term *snooping?*"

She crossed her arms and leaned against the counter. He said, "Okay, here goes. Chances are I was looking for the same thing you've been looking for. That is, some evidence that might lead to whoever cooked the books at your father's company."

"My father didn't do it," she said flatly.

"Neither did Will."

They eyed each other warily. When Mac found his thoughts straying in another direction, he turned and stacked the few dishes in the drainer and ran water over them. "If we're going to talk, you need to sit down. Lying down would be even better, because whether or not you want to admit it, lady, you're bushed."

This time she couldn't stifle her yawn. Still yawning, she wandered away, and moments later he heard her sigh as she settled onto the sofa. He was tempted to join her, to fold the duvet around her, massage her shoulders and finish up by rubbing lotion into those red, rough hands.

After drying his own hands, he rolled down his sleeves and joined her. "All right, start talking," she said before he could frame his first question.

Sergeant Valerie. Make that General.

"Like I said, I'm looking for the same thing you are. Makes sense to me to pool our resources." He waited for a reaction. While he watched, she closed her eyes and grimaced.

"What?" he said.

"Cramp." The word came through clenched teeth. She started to stand, but he was up before she could get both feet on the floor.

"Where? Your calf? Right or left?"

"Foot. Right one."

By the time he'd slipped off her shoe and bent her toes toward her body, then worked the sole of her foot between his hands, she was lying back on the sofa, eyes closed, groaning in either pleasure or pain, he couldn't be certain which.

"I think that's got it," she whispered.

"Anything else?" He held his hands up as if he were a surgeon scrubbed for an operation.

She looked at his raised hands and almost smiled. Almost, but not quite. "I shouldn't," she said. "We really do need to talk."

"We can talk tomorrow, tell me what else hurts."

"I have to go to work tomorrow."

"Valerie, what's hurting? You can't tackle another cleaning job if your muscles freeze up on you."

Instead of answering, she rolled over onto her stomach and twitched one shoulder. It was all the invitation he needed.

Eventually she said lethargically, "I still have a bone to pick with you. Ahh…right there."

It was weakness on her part, sheer self-indulgence, but Val let him work his magic on her aching shoulders. When his hands moved to her lower back, she couldn't find the energy to protest. By morning, that would probably have stiffened up, too. Crawling around on her knees, dragging junk out from under furniture. A single wading shoe. Two used paper plates. A kid's snorkel.

She sighed again. They had come to some sort of an agreement…hadn't they? And honestly, she rationalized, it made sense. What one person saw as insignificant, another pair of eyes might see as vitally important.

"Two brains are better than one," she murmured sleepily.

His hands slowed, circled her shoulders, his thumbs now working at the rigid deltoids. Where had it all come from—the tension? It couldn't be simply the result of cleaning one filthy cottage and two fairly clean ones. Red hands and sore knees, sure, but tension?

He leaned over and inhaled. She could feel his breath on her cheek, her neck. "Your hair smells like ginger lilies. I think."

Without opening her eyes, she smiled. "You think?"

"White flowers. Grow in Florida. Smell sweet, not at all like ginger?"

"Close enough," she managed to whisper just before she felt his lips on her nape. *Oh, please don't do that. I don't have the strength to resist....*

He backed away, bumped against the coffee table and one of the files slid to the floor. Neither of them noticed. When he scooped her up in his arms, Val made a weak protest, but both of them knew they were past that point. Logical or not—timely or not, he was going to do what she had dreamed about ever since that kiss on the beach. Ever since they had huddled out of the rain in a deserted shelter, his body pressing hers against the wall, her arms around his waist, her hands cupping his lean buttocks.

Nothing else in her life made any sense—why should this?

Ten

Mac wanted to carry her upstairs, but Val insisted on being set on her feet. As the steps were too narrow, they jostled their way to the top, arms around waists, hips nudging hips, hearts pounding as one.

At least, hers was. As she wasn't wearing a bra—didn't really need one—her feather-soft sweatshirt moved against her sensitized nipples until all she could think of was tearing off her clothes and feeling his hands on her body, his lips—

It's going to happen, a voice inside her whispered. *Don't fight it.*

Another voice answered, *Who's fighting?* Something told her it was now or never, and never wasn't even a faint possibility.

Her bed was a double and her mattress was in

somewhat better condition than his, but he could have taken her on any floor in the house, sandy or not, and she wouldn't have complained as long as he joined her there.

She felt for the overhead light switch just inside the door, but he stayed her hand. Instead, he turned on the hall light and left the door ajar. Just as well. She was hardly a centerfold candidate.

And while she was not without experience, she suddenly felt awkward. Unlike the polished sophisticate she'd nearly married, and the tennis club gigolo she'd briefly fallen for, Mac was a real man in every sense of the word. What if he was disappointed? She would die if he looked at her flat chest and said something like, "Where's the beef?"

Tripp had said that once, then laughed as if he'd been only teasing. Looking back, she realized that Tripp's brand of teasing had almost always held a hidden barb.

"Val? It's not too late," Mac said, but of course it was. It had been too late the first time she'd seen him standing in the middle of her front yard like a conquering hero looking over the spoils of war.

"I know that," she snapped. So much for lifelong lessons in deportment. She couldn't even manage a simple seduction scene with any style.

Reaching for the drawstring at her waist, she looked at him as if to say, *I will if you will.*

Stepping out of his shoes, Mac's gaze never left her face. He unbuttoned his fly—he wasn't wearing a belt. *You first,* those whiskey-brown eyes dared.

Boldly, she stepped out of her pants, then quickly tugged the bottom of the pink sweatshirt down over her hips. If he liked big-bosomed women, he was flat out of luck, *flat* being the operative word.

Judging from the way he stepped out of his pants, tossed them onto a chair and pulled his Columbia U sweatshirt over his head, self-consciousness wasn't even in his vocabulary. If briefs came in cup sizes, his would be a double-D.

He caught her staring. "Val? If you've changed your mind, just say so. But don't wait too long...please?"

Frantically, she shook her head. Oh, for goodness sake—thirty years old and you'd think she'd never done it before.

But standing there in his navy briefs, his thick, sunstreaked hair awry, he looked so heartbreakingly beautiful she wanted to weep. Instead, she tugged off her shirt, stepped out of her panties and confronted him, daring him to back out.

When he closed his eyes her heart sank. Then he stepped out of his briefs and stood there, fully aroused, but still not touching her. Her mouth was dry. Other parts were embarrassingly wet. "Well, are we going to do this or not?" she demanded belligerently.

At least it broke the tension. He laughed unsteadily and reached for her. If she didn't know better, she might even believe he was as nervous as she was. Together they made it onto the bed, and Val told herself it would be all right. This was Mac—she trusted him.

Don't think about tomorrow. Don't think, just live the moment.

"I don't want to hurt you," he said.

"I'm hardly fragile." When his flattened palms made small circles on her nipples, she caught her breath.

"Yeah, you are. Lucky for you, I'm good at handling beautiful, priceless, fragile treasures."

It was the last word either of them spoke for a while. He kissed her then, a gentle exploration that quickly escalated to a carnal assault. As if the taste of him weren't intoxicating enough, the feel of his arousal pulsing against her drove her out of her mind with need.

"Please," she managed to whisper. "Now?"

He murmured something that she was beyond hearing, much less understanding, and left her briefly. Moments later he returned. He kissed her eyes, her nose, her chin, and then moved down her throat and beyond, his hands leading the way, his lips following. She could feel her small breasts swell under the gentle assault from his tongue as he sucked her nipples, then gently grazed them with his teeth. All the while his hands were moving on her body, tracing erotic patterns on her most sensitive flesh.

Digging into his shoulders with her fingertips, she twisted her head on the pillow, whimpering as he carried her to new heights, leading her to the very brink and back again and again. Stunned with sheer sensation, she was barely able to breathe. By the time he settled himself between her parted thighs, her fists were gripping the sheets to keep her from soaring into orbit.

He entered her slowly. Impatiently, she thrust her hips to meet him, urging him to hurry. Braced on his elbows, he was trembling, his face the face of a stranger.

A stranger…

Before second thoughts could wedge their way between them he slipped his hand down her body and touched her in a way that jolted her into final orbit. "Shh, easy," he whispered, but his voice was unsteady.

Slowly, he moved deeply inside her. Clenching her thighs around his waist, she moved frantically to meet his thrusts. They were wildly out of synch, but it didn't seem to matter—didn't matter at all, as wave after wave of pulsating pleasure washed over her.

She shuddered, caught her breath and released it in a soft scream. Never…*ever*…had she flown this high! Not until the last sweet, heavy ring of sensation faded, leaving behind a deep, mellow ache, did it occur to her that she still couldn't breathe.

She must have made some sound because Mac shifted his weight and rolled onto his side, taking her with him. "Sorry," he muttered. "I died for a few minutes."

Petit mort. The small death…

As reluctant as she was to move, Val felt her defenses click into place. She felt a desperate need to prove that what just happened meant no more to her than it had to him.

Simple sex, she reasoned. People did it all the time.

Simple? Pompeii had been simple. The San Francisco earthquake had been simple. Sex with MacBride was anything *but* simple.

He was stirring against her again…down there. She was tempted just for a moment, but then common sense prevailed. "This is all very well, but I need to get some sleep," she said shrewishly. "I have to go to work tomorrow."

He stared at her as if not believing what he'd just heard.

She couldn't believe she'd said it. Oh, God, how utterly awful. It was no less than the truth, but far from the whole truth. If they did it again, he might fall asleep in her bed, and if they spent an entire night together, nuzzling, nestling, making love again and again, she might never allow him to escape. Too weak to make it down to the kitchen, they would eventually starve. Sometime in the distant future Marian would send someone to check on her, and there they'd be—two naked skeletons, bones entwined on a rumpled bed.

Carefully, she disentangled herself, then pretended to be asleep. The moment she felt him ease out of bed, she opened one eye. God, he was gorgeous!

"Want me to bring up an alarm clock?" he asked. Obviously he hadn't bought her pretense of sleep.

Nor was he the least bit self-conscious about his nudity.

"No thanks," she said coolly, watching as he casually scooped up his clothes and left. When he was halfway to the stairs, she called after him. "Yes— would you mind? Just set it on the dresser."

Mac let the cold shower drill down on him for several minutes. He was deep in uncharted waters without a tank, without so much as a snorkel. His left brain had shut down completely—he couldn't have reasoned his way out of a coat closet. As for his right brain, it kept creating these crazy images of big, soft beds and a certain slender, soft woman. A woman he'd come down here to entrap, only nothing was turning out the way he'd expected. He could no longer even pretend to be objective. Peel off the surface patina and Valerie Bonnard, heiress and socialite, was as real as any woman shoving a basket through the supermarket with two kids hanging onto her skirt. Same basic hopes, same basic fears— maybe even dreams, although she hadn't shared those with him.

Instead, she had shared her body.

And now he found himself picturing a half-grown boy with dark hair and eyes the color of damp Spanish moss diving beside him, while just offstage a little girl in a white tutu and red ballerina shoes tried out a few classic moves.

Shutting off the water, he stepped out of the shower and toweled off, still picturing those long legs. She had a slight tendency to knock knees that probably bothered her, but it sure as hell didn't bother him. Her hips flared nicely—that much he'd noticed in those jeans she wore under all the layers on top. Her breasts were barely a palmful, the nipples dark and proud, as if begging for his attention.

Jeez, at this rate he'd need another cold shower, Mac told himself, reaching for the boxers he slept in.

There was an alarm clock in the kitchen. It was set for seven. He left it that way and headed back upstairs. She was feigning sleep when he let himself into her bedroom, Baby Ben in hand. He let her get away with it. Morning would come soon enough, and by then he needed his mind to be completely clear.

Or at least marginally functional.

Downstairs again, he glanced at his watch. It was barely ten o'clock. He had plenty of time to tackle a few more of those frustrating files, knowing she wouldn't come downstairs again before morning.

But that would be cheating, and suddenly, he couldn't do that any longer. "Hell of a position you put yourself in, MacBride."

He swore softly, checked the front door and then headed toward the back of the house. If you can sleep, lady, then so can I, he thought grimly. But the first time he heard her bed so much as squeak overhead, he'd be out of there and up those stairs so fast his feet would strike sparks on the worn old treads.

In other words, fellow, you're down for the count.

Val opened her eyes moments before the clock went off and lay awake, thinking of those enigmatic scribbles she'd found on so many of the papers in her father's files. Initials, single numbers, sums—random, seemingly meaningless words. If it was a code of some kind, he should have given her the key.

She showered, thinking of Mac's enclosed stall downstairs. She pictured him standing there, his naked body with its generous dusting of dark hair gleaming wetly.

"Stop it. Just stop that!" she muttered, roughly toweling her hair before snatching up her blow-dryer.

She had two more cottages to clean before she could get started on the files again. One had to be done this morning, the other could wait, as it wasn't booked, but she might as well do it anyway. She needed the money, and besides, she hated having anything hanging over her head. Anything more than she already had.

Over breakfast, which Mac had waiting for her some twenty minutes later, he announced his intention of helping her clean.

"Last night we agreed to tackle the files together," he reminded her. "Same thing applies to the cleaning. We'll get it done faster and then we can come back here and concentrate on those files."

Last night she would have agreed to jump through a ring of fire. Today she was back in control. "I can do it and be back here in two hours. In the meanwhile, you might want to—to—" She couldn't think of another chore that needed doing at the moment. At least none he was capable of that she could afford.

She said, "My showerhead. It drizzles. I prefer a needle spray."

"Hard-water deposits. I'll soak it out while we're cleaning your cottages."

She slanted him a skeptical look. "You're not going to give up, are you?" She'd counted on spending a few hours away in hopes that she might be able to restore a few of her defenses.

"A handyman does what a handyman has to do." He had the nerve to grin at her.

"Fine," she snapped. "I'll pay you half of what I get paid."

But nothing was fine, she thought. Her whole orderly life had been turned into a gigantic roller coaster. All she could do was hang on and hope it would eventually come to rest.

He insisted on driving, so she got out the map Marian had given her and directed him to the road that ended in two soundside cottages. Traffic was light. They'd passed a car and two trucks, one of them towing a boat bigger than it was before Mac said, "Look, about last night. I want you to know—"

"I don't want to talk about it. It happened, it's finished, just forget it. That one with the white trim— that's one of them."

They finished well under the allotted time. Mac insisted on doing the vacuuming and mopping floors while she cleaned the bathrooms. Four of them, with only three bedrooms. If she'd learned one thing in the brief time she'd been living in her great-grandmother's house it was that the quality of life had little to do with the standard of living.

"Can you think of a single reason why someone would go off and leave a vegetable drawer full of cosmetics and a kitchen garbage can half full of dead oysters?'' she asked as they pulled up before her house less a few hours later. "Should I get the address from Marian and mail the woman her cosmetics?''

"Toss the cosmetics and mail her the oysters.''

She bit back a snort of laughter and opened the door.

"Go sit,'' Mac ordered once they were inside. The house smelled slightly of vinegar. "I'll rinse out your showerhead and reinstall it, then I'll fix us something to eat.''

"Don't spoil me,'' she said, dropping wearily onto a chair.

"Don't tempt me.'' He flashed her a quick grin as he poured the bowl of white vinegar down the drain and ran fresh water through the showerhead.

A few minutes later he made them both sandwiches. She sat and watched him layer on cheese and pastrami while he told her about the concretions he'd left in Will's garage, some soaked free and carefully pried apart, others still in their natural state.

She followed him into the living room feeling spoiled and just a wee bit decadent, being waited on by a man like MacBride. He carried the tray. She carried the paper napkins.

"Got an idea," he said after consuming half his sandwich in three bites.

"What, more mustard? You used half a jar."

"About your dad's hieroglyphics. I don't think it's stock symbols, I think it's someone's initials. Who do you know whose initials are M.L.?"

"Nobody. I've thought and thought about it, but that doesn't necessarily mean anything. I didn't know half the people who worked at BFC."

Mac had watched her eat. For a lady who probably knew her way around a six-fork table setting, she had a healthy appetite. In more respects than one, he thought, feeling his heart kick into a higher gear. She left the pickle till last. When she started nibbling on the tip, he stood and snatched up her plate. "I'll just, uh—go put the food away. You want to wash up before we get started?"

She avoided his eyes, and it occurred to Mac that she might even be thinking about the same thing he was remembering in intricate detail. To get them both back on track, he repeated his suspicions as soon as he rejoined her in the living room with coffee for him, hot tea for her. "M stands for Mitty?"

"M. L., not M. S. Miss Mitty's name is Matilda, but her last name is Stoddard. And anyway, she couldn't possibly be involved because we knew her forever. At least since the middle eighties when BFC was incorporated."

"Everybody knows somebody." For a woman he knew to be highly intelligent, she was incredibly naive. "This accountant who left, what are his initials?"

"Hers. P. T. I thought about her, too, but I don't remember seeing those initials."

They went through the names of everyone on the executive floor and a few of the lower echelon, only three of whom had been there since the beginning. Of the three, Mitty Stoddard, was gone. Frank Bonnard was dead, and that left—

"You're sure about Hutchinson? I know he was questioned and finally cleared, but someone ripped off all those people, and it wasn't Will Jordan, I'd stake my life on it."

"It wasn't my father, either. I've known him all my life." She shook her head, muttered, "Duh," and then said, "Look, integrity is something a person either has or he doesn't. It's not a—a situational thing. If my father picked up a dime on the sidewalk, he'd look around to see if he could find who might have dropped it."

A dime, maybe, but several million dollars?

Mac sighed. "Back to square one. M. L. shows up more than any other set of initials, right? So let's see what else we can find, and this time check out the context. Remember, it doesn't have to be someone who's been there from the beginning, it could easily be a new hire…only not too new."

"Like your brother."

Ignoring the comment, he lifted three files from the box and placed them on the coffee table. "By the way, where did you say this friend of yours moved to when she left Greenwich?''

''Miss Mitty? Monroe, Georgia. She has a niece there.'' Val's eyes held a warning glint, but she didn't argue.

''You happen to know the niece's name?''

''It's Brown—Rebecca Brown. I have the phone number.''

She could have refused to cooperate. By now she had to know that someone was going to get roughed up before they were finished. He said, ''Look, if you're determined to clear your father's name, it's a case of no holds barred.''

''Holes?''

''Holds. Don't you ever watch wrestling?''

She rolled her eyes, and it served as well as anything could to break the tension. She picked up a folder, spread the papers on the table and pointed to the distinctive turquoise-colored ink. ''M. L. again. And there's a date.''

For the next few hours they went over page after page, noting context as much as what had been written across the face of the various documents. By the time Val had yawned half a dozen times, Mac was pretty sure he knew where the trail was going to end. Now all he had to do was figure out the best way to follow it, because suspicions alone weren't enough.

''Come on, let's call it a night.''

Eleven

Neither of them bothered to pretend they weren't going to end up in bed together. In matters concerning BFC they might be skating on thin ice over moving water, but when it came to personal matters, Val couldn't even pretend to hold back. What had happened before—spontaneous combustion described it best—might have been ill-conceived, but she'd be lying if she said she didn't want it to happen again...and again.

"Shower's all ready to go," Mac told her. "If you need any help, just yell." He stopped at the bathroom door, leaned back against the wall and drew her into his arms. It was a long time before she reluctantly stepped away.

"You might smooth the bed. I don't think I ever got around to making it today."

"Yes, ma'am. Anything else, Miss B.?" The devil lurked in his clear brown eyes. She loved it when he teased her this way.

"Wait for me on the left side of the bed. I always sleep on the right."

"Who said anything about sleeping?" He leaned in for one last kiss, then opened the bathroom door.

Laughing, she said, "Five minutes. Oh, and Mac…be naked."

It took her four. One minute to splash off, one to dry, one to smooth on a layer of body lotion, and one to hurry across the cool bare floors to the bedroom. By the time she opened the door she was scarcely breathing. *Am I stark, raving mad?* she wondered, staring at the dim pink-lit room. He had found her peach-and-black Hermés scarf and draped it over the lamp on the dresser. Lying on his back in the center of the bed, arms crossed under his head, he was grinning like a drunken satyr.

"Last one in's a rotten egg," he jeered softly. She dropped the towel, darted across the floor and dived onto the bed. He caught her, laughing, and pulled her on top of him.

Not until much later, when she collapsed in a damp heap, every nerve ending in her body still tingling, did she manage to speak. "Mine's the superior position, you'll notice."

"I noticed." The sleepy look he sent her could

easily be described as a leer. "Just try it without me and see how superior you feel."

"Mmm, now that you mention it, I believe further research might be called for."

Between sessions of serious research they managed to sleep for a few hours. Eventually Mac got up and turned off the light, saying something about a fire hazard.

Any fire hazard, Val remembered thinking, was here in bed, not across the room on the dresser. She awoke sometime in the middle of the night with her head on Mac's shoulder, one knee curled up over his thigh and her hand dangerously near ground zero.

Carefully, she eased it away. She needed to go to the bathroom, and if she'd learned anything at all last night it was that Mac had a low threshold of arousal. Almost as low as her own.

Another thing she'd learned, with decidedly mixed emotions, was that she was deeply, irredeemably in love, and it felt nothing at all like the few other times she'd thought she was in love.

Not that love was going to prevent her from doing what she'd come down here to do. Today they were going to go over those damned files with a magnifying glass, if necessary. Mac was determined to find something he could interpret as proof of his stepbrother's innocence, never mind that it might seal her father's guilt for all time. That done, he would leave. Mission accomplished. Damn the torpedoes, full speed ahead as an Annapolis cadet she'd once dated used to quote whenever he downed one drink too many.

Okay, he was a lover and leaver. She could handle it. "What the dickens does a marine archeologist know about criminology, anyway? Or accounting, for that matter?"

The belligerent face in the bathroom mirror issued a reply. "About as much as an art history major with a minor in English lit."

Mac waited until he heard the shower running before collecting his clothes and heading downstairs. He had a feeling he was in deeper water than he was rated for. Decompression was going to be a problem, if it was even possible. One place to start was with a phone call to his hacker friend Shirley, and another one was to an old diving buddy who was currently working with the Atlanta PD Special Crimes Unit.

He showered, dressed, placed both calls and was frying bacon when Val made the scene. The first thing he noticed was that she was wearing makeup and one of those fancy outfits that was probably supposed to look casual. White chamois pants, several loose layers of cashmere and silk, with shirttails dangling. Her hair was twisted up in a knot and she'd taken time to put on makeup.

He could have commented, but he chose not to in case she happened to be feeling as vulnerable as he was. He could afford to allow her whatever armor she thought she needed. Hell, he might even have joined in the masquerade, only he'd left his formal wear back in Mystic. Three ties, a navy blazer and a pair of khakis that still held a crease.

"Scrambled or fried?"

She shuddered. "Tea and toast," she said, and as soon as he set the food on the table, proceeded to filch bacon off his plate until he got up and handed her a plate and a fork. "Help me out here, I scrambled enough eggs for a platoon."

They finished breakfast, mostly in silence, and then he said, "Leave the dishes. Come on in the living room, I think we're on the verge of a breakthrough."

Three-quarters of an hour and half a pot of coffee later, the second of the corroborating phone calls came through. Mac had also talked to Will while Val had been showering. Now, surrounded by open files, the documents sorted in chronological order, he took the second call, allowing Val to hear his sparse responses. Her lipstick had been chewed off, and the blush on her cheeks stood out against her pallor.

"Uh-huh," he said. "Gotcha."

Damn, he hated this. If there was any way he could have spared her, he'd have done it, even at Will's expense. That was a sign of just how deep these particular waters were.

But the evidence was damning. The trail had been carefully followed and just as carefully concealed by a man who'd been clever, but far too softhearted until it was too late. Bonnard would've soon turned over the evidence, Mac was certain of it, only there hadn't been time.

There was no way to make this any easier for her. It never even occurred to him that she might not believe him without proof. As unlikely as it was, especially under the circumstances, a deep level of trust had grown between them. She was as aware of it as he was, even when they bickered over details.

He pressed the off button, laid his phone aside and stared out the window, stroking his chin between thumb and forefinger. She had to know what he'd been leading up to. The only thing that had been lacking was the identity of M. L., the initials that had turned up on more than half her father's papers.

Finally, she said, "What?"

"Honey, you're not going to like this."

"Mac, you're scaring me."

He eased her over on the sofa and sat down beside her. "Matilda Lyford. Did your friend ever tell you she'd been married?"

She stopped breathing, shaking her head slowly. "Miss Mitty, you mean," she whispered.

"In eighty-seven, Matilda Stoddard married Vernon Lyford. The marriage took place in Morganton, West Virginia, and lasted approximately three weeks. Lyford was jailed on a check-kiting scam. Meanwhile, the bride moved gradually northeast, spending eighteen months working with a mortgage bank in Cumberland, Maryland, and another few months as a receptionist with a medical insurance firm in Philadelphia. Both times she left under—I guess you might say under a cloud. By the time she arrived in Greenwich, she'd reverted to her maiden name, although there's no record of her ever having it legally changed. For that matter, there's no record of a divorce.''

''Mitty Stoddard,'' Val whispered.

Mac nodded. ''Honey, I'm afraid your Miss Mitty wasn't all she pretended to be. She'd be how old when she married, late fifties?''

Val nodded, her eyes suspiciously bright. ''You never met her, but Mac, she was everyone's idea of the perfect grandmother. Gray hair, lace-up shoes, plastic-rimmed bifocals. Back when everyone else was wearing granny glasses, I remember hearing her say that they were fine for the young, but not for any woman past middle age. She went to church. She— she—'' Swallowing hard, she shook her head and whispered, ''I can't believe it.''

Mac drew her head down on his shoulder and covered her hands with his. His were tanned and callused. Hers were rough, with the beginning of a rash. God, he loved this woman, dishpan hands, smeared mascara and all.

''Your father knew.'' Even though Bonnard had not been the embezzler, he'd been Stoddard's employer, and as such, a target for liability suits. No point in bringing that up now, though. ''He probably hated to confront her, but he'd have done it, Val. That's why he was collecting evidence.''

She laughed brokenly. ''Evidence? If that was supposed to be evidence, then why did he hide it? Why not just tell someone about his suspicions?''

''Because suspicions alone aren't enough. Before he accused an old friend, he had to be dead certain. Sooner or later he'd have gone to the authorities.''

''Only later never happened,'' she whispered.

''Best I can figure, Matilda Stoddard, or whatever she called herself, had been inventing retirees, settling up accounts and shifting the money to another account for at least a couple of years. Some of the initials could represent different banks, or maybe fictitious accounts. As for the sums, add a couple of zeros and that probably represents a pretty accurate figure for each phony account.''

Once they knew what to look for it became all too clear. Matilda Lyford, complete with at least two different social security numbers—possibly others, as well, had set up four separate bank accounts, careful to keep each transaction under the limit of ten thousand dollars, which would have automatically flagged the transaction.

''And nobody ever figured out what was going on,'' Val murmured.

''Because no one was looking for it. A few thousand a month here, a few thousand there—after a while it adds up to a pretty nice package. Especially once she started scooping up real money.''

''Just before she retired, you mean.''

''Couple of months. Probably figured by the time anyone caught on she'd be out of there.''

''She was right,'' Val said with a shuddering sigh.

Almost a sigh of relief. "Mac, it hurts. No one likes to be wrong about people, but..."

"On the other hand, sometimes being wrong is just fine." His look said it all. He leaned over and tipped her face up for a quick kiss. Quick only because they still had some ground to cover before he headed north with the collected evidence to turn it over to the authorities.

"I take it you know where she is now," Val said, obviously determined to get every painful detail over before the anesthesia wore off.

"Florida. One of the better retirement communities. Fancy apartment, water aerobics, weekly concerts, trips to Disneyland and Sea World. At a minimum rate of about eight grand a month she'd be set for a long, comfortable retirement. Instead..."

"Do you mind if we don't talk about it any more?"

"Nope. I think we both pretty well accomplished our missions. Will's in the clear. Your dad's reputation is restored. In fact, he'll wind up being something of a hero for having figured out what was going on. If he'd lived, he'd have taken his evidence to the authorities, and you and I would never have met. Will's wife would never have left him—yeah, well, maybe she would, at that."

"Go back." She was rubbing his knuckles, then letting her fingers trace the length of each finger.

"To Greenwich? To Mystic?"

Then she came up on her knees beside him and

shoved her face close to his. "Back to where you said we wouldn't have met. Betcha you're wrong."

He caught on pretty fast when it came to shipwrecks and women he loved. "Betcha you're right."

She said, "Prove it."

And he did.

Epilogue

She knew he was there, but refused to turn around.
She'd heard him drive up. The old Land Cruiser was
going to need a new muffler before long. Beach driving was rough on vehicles.

Imagine my knowing that, Val thought, amused.
She turned slightly and aimed the stream of water on
the other Cape jasmine. It got a tad more sun now
that Mac had trimmed a few branches. Both of them
were coming along nicely.

She felt his breath on her nape a second before
she felt his lips. "You shouldn't be out here in this
heat," he scolded.

Dropping the hose, she turned and let herself be
folded into her husband's embrace—which wasn't as
easy as it had been only a few weeks ago.

"Any luck?" she asked after being thoroughly kissed.

"Not yet." In his free time her husband and a local historian were trying to get a lead on a schooner that had gone down more than a hundred years ago in the mouth of Hatteras Inlet. Neither of them seriously expected to find anything, but Mac enjoyed a challenge.

"Ever the optimist," she teased.

"You bet. Look what optimism got me."

When he went over to shut off the hose, Val thought dreamily—she spent a lot of time these days in that state—about the fact that neither of their worst fears had been realized.

Which reminded her— "Will called," she said. "He insisted he doesn't want to impose, but I insisted right back. He can have the back rooms." Along with the rest of the house, those had been refinished and refurbished. "How good is he at painting ceilings?"

Mac laughed. They were finishing up the nursery. Marian Kuvarky had brought over a sack of baby clothes and offered to help with the trim. He had a feeling his stepbrother might be in for a surprise if Val's machinations bore fruit. He liked the real estate agent just fine, but he didn't know if poor Will was ready for any matchmaking.

"You hungry?" he asked, leading his bride of nine months inside the yellow house with the neat black shutters.

"Always," she answered with a ladylike version

of a leer. "One more month, and then six more weeks after that."

He chuckled. "Six inches or twelve?"

"Twelve. I'm starved."

They always had subs on Wednesdays. On Mondays and Fridays, Mac grilled fish. Val had discovered several new talents, but cooking wasn't among them.

"I joined another group today," she told him with a sly grin.

"That makes one for every day of the week. What's this one, Mothers Against Toe-dancing?"

She elbowed him in the ribs and adjusted the thermometer. The heat pump had been one of her wedding gifts from her bridegroom. "Genealogy, smartmouth. This baby of ours has cousins out the wazoo."

"I keep warning you, you're going to have to clean up your act, honey. Ladies don't use vulgar terms like *wazoo*."

"Guess what else ladies don't do," she teased.

"Afraid to ask." Already grinning in anticipation, Mac tossed his baseball cap onto the coat tree she had found at the local thrift shop.

"Come on upstairs and I'll show you."

Besotted, he followed her swaying backside up the narrow stairway, thinking vague thoughts of sea sirens and tiny ballerinas.

Supper could wait....

* * * * *

**is proud to present the first in the
provocative new miniseries**

DYNASTIES : THE DANFORTHS

*A family of prominence...
tested by scandal,
sustained by passion!*

---

with

The Cinderella Scandal
by BARBARA
McCAULEY

Tina Alexander's life changed when
handsome Reid Danforth walked into
her family bakery with heated gazes aimed
only at her! They soon fell into bed...but
neither lover was all that they seemed.
Would hidden scandals put an end to
their fiery fairy-tale romance?

*Available January 2004
at your favorite retail outlet.*

Silhouette® Desire®

presents

KING OF HEARTS

You're on his hit list.

Enjoy the next title in

KATHERINE GARBERA's

King of Hearts miniseries:

Let It Ride

(Silhouette Desire #1558)

With the help of a matchmaking
angel in training, a cynical casino owner
gambles his heart to win the love
of a picture-perfect bride.

*Available January 2004
at your favorite retail outlet.*

The Stolen Baby

Silhouette Desire's powerful miniseries features six wealthy Texas bachelors—all members of the state's most prestigious club—who set out to unravel the mystery surrounding one tiny baby...and discover true love in the process!

This newest installment continues with,

Remembering One Wild Night

by KATHIE DeNOSKY

(Silhouette Desire #1559)

Meet Travis Whelan—a jet-setting attorney... and a *father*? When Natalie Perez showed up in his life again with the baby daughter he'd never known about, Travis knew he had a duty to both of them. But could he find a way to make them a family?

Available January 2004 at your favorite retail outlet.

Nora's extraordinary Donovan family is back!

#1 *New York Times* bestselling author

NORA ROBERTS

Captivated

The Donovans remain one of Nora Roberts's most unforgettable families. For along with their irresistible appeal they've inherited some rather remarkable gifts from their Celtic ancestors. In this classic story Nash Kirkland falls under the bewitching spell of mysterious Morgana Donovan.

Available in February at your favorite retail outlet.

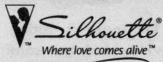

Silhouette®

Where love comes alive™

The Wolfe twins' stories—
together in one fantastic volume!

USA TODAY bestselling author

JOAN
HOHL
Double
WOLFE

The emotional story of Matilda Wolfe plus an original short
story about Matilda's twin sister, Lisa. The twins have
followed different paths...but each leads to true love!

Look for DOUBLE WOLFE in January 2004.

"A compelling storyteller who weaves her tales
with verve, passion and style."
—*New York Times* bestselling author Nora Roberts

Where love comes alive™

COMING NEXT MONTH

#1555 THE CINDERELLA SCANDAL—Barbara McCauley
Dynasties: The Danforths
Tina Alexander had always lived in the shadows of her gorgeous sisters, so imagine her surprise when Reid Danforth walked into her family bakery with heated gazes aimed only at her! Soon the two fell into bed—and into an unexpected relationship. But would this Cinderella's hidden scandal put an end to their fairy-tale romance?

#1556 FULL THROTTLE—Merline Lovelace
To Protect and Defend
Paired together for a top secret test mission, scientist Kate Hargrave and U.S. Air Force Captain Dave Scott clashed from the moment they met, setting off sparks with every conflict. Would it be only a matter of time before Kate gave in to Dave's advances…and discovered a physical attraction neither would know how to walk away from?

#1557 MIDNIGHT SEDUCTION—Justine Davis
Redstone, Incorporated
An inheritance and a cryptic note led Emma Purcell to the Pacific Northwest—and to sexy Harlen McClaren. As Emma and Harlen unraveled the mystery left behind by her late cousin, pent-up passions came to life, taking over their senses…and embedding them in the deepest mystery of all: love!

#1558 LET IT RIDE—Katherine Garbera
King of Hearts
Vacationing in Vegas was exactly what Kylie Smith needed. The lights! The casinos! The quickie marriages? Billionaire casino owner Deacon Prescott spotted Kylie on the security monitor and knew the picture of domesticity would be perfect as his wife: Prim in public, passionate in private. But was Deacon prepared to get more than he bargained for?

#1559 REMEMBERING ONE WILD NIGHT—Kathie DeNosky
Texas Cattleman's Club: The Stolen Baby
Waking from amnesia, single mother Natalie Perez knew her child was in danger. High-powered lawyer Travis Whelan was the only man who could protect her daughter—the man who had lied to her and broken her heart…and the father of her baby. Would the wild attraction they shared overcome past betrayals and unite them as a family?

#1560 AT YOUR SERVICE—Amy Jo Cousins
Runaway heiress Grace Haley donned an apron and posed as a waitress while trying to get out from under her powerful—and manipulative—family's thumb. Grace just wanted a chance to figure out her life. Instead she found herself sparring with her boss, sexy pub owner Christopher Tyler, and soon her hands were full of more than just dishes.…

SDCNM1203